stories by

JOHN WYNNE

city lights

SAN FRANCISCO

Acknowledgments:
I would like to thank my editor, Amy Scholder, for her support
and creative expertise.

Cover design by Rex Ray
Book design by Amy Scholder
Typography by Harvest Graphics

Library of Congress Cataloging-in-Publication Data

Wynne, John (John Stewart)
      The other world : short stories / by John Wynne.
          p.   cm.
      ISBN 0-87286-290-9 : $9.95
      1. Gay men — Fiction.   I. Title.
   PS3573.Y627087   1994
   813'.54 — dc20   94-7407
                                                               CIP

City Lights Books are available to bookstores through our primary
distributor: Subterranean Company, P. O. Box 168, 265 S. 5th St.,
Monroe, OR 97456. 503-847-5274. Toll-free orders 800-274-7826.
FAX 503-847-6018. Our books are also available through library
jobbers and regional distributors. For personal orders and catalogs,
please write to City Lights Books, 261 Columbus Avenue,
San Francisco, CA 94133.

CITY LIGHTS BOOKS are edited by Lawrence Ferlinghetti and
Nancy J. Peters and published at the City Lights Bookstore,
261 Columbus Avenue, San Francisco, CA 94133.

Dedicated to Stephen Adams

and in memory of Michael Turner-Holden

and to Harold Schmidt

with deep appreciation

for his heartfelt enthusiasm

Contents

THE OTHER WORLD

THE GROCERY CARTS WERE SCATTERED OVER THE LOT. HE could already feel his hands forced against the hot bars. *Goddam people,* Pete thought, *leave 'em anywhere.* He packed the last sack with bananas, cereal, and Cokes. Then he glanced up at the booth and, of course, Mr. Raney was giving him the nod. Pete nodded back, wiped his hands on his apron and stepped outside. The sun hit him full in the face. He couldn't find a breath of air that wasn't wet or heavy or yellow. He started rounding up the carts. The scenery wasn't so bad today. A band of girls was heading home from the Dairy Queen. They carried foamy whipped sodas and chocolate-dipped cones. They wore shorts. Tight. Their legs had soft white hairs. He liked one of the girls. Ruby Lacy. Her tongue darted out to save the melting chocolate. He felt his stomach get all tight. He jerked the baskets away from the Buick just in time, but the old man still yelled, "Watch where you're goin', will ya?" Back inside, Pete chose to stock the canned milk so he could bend down and see up the girls' skirts. Ray was left with the higher shelves. "Better keep the radio down, old man Raney might come around any minute." But Ray kept flipping stations. Sweet and creamy pop sounds. There was a special song he was looking for. Something about love on a rooftop. "That's a real old one," Pete insisted. "No, it ain't. I hear it in the halls at school all

1

the time." "Just keep it way low . . ." Canned milk cans. Pete wiped his forehead.

At dinner no one spoke much. Florence wiped the pudding off Michael's chin. "Mom," Pete said. Florence smiled and raised her head. "How long usually before a first paycheck?" She fed another spoonful to the baby. "I don't know, dear. I just don't know." Pete stared. He hated her hair that way, those thin beige strands swept up into an old-fashioned bun. His father finished his ham steak. His brother, James, sat dreaming into space. "I mowed the entire lawn today," Rich Grady said. "You boys can do the trimming. Is it a deal?" "Sure, Dad." "Yeah, Dad." Pete thought bitterly that James didn't even have a summer job — why, he should do all the trimming himself. "Where is Carol tonight?" Florence asked James. "She's studying for her biology exam." "That girl is such a good student." Florence got the last of the bean pudding down the baby's throat.

At ten, Pete wasn't sleepy. There wasn't much to read except the encyclopedia. He chose *Vol. 15 MARY to MUS* and almost choked when he came upon a big color picture of MODERN DRAMATIC MASKS — "Mural paintings by Wladyslaw T. Benda showing the dramatic use of masks as they are employed in grotesque painting." His blood swelled, his heart beat swiftly. There was a naked woman surrounded by eight creatures and a lion. But the eight creatures were part human. Pete was stunned to see some had webbed feet and hands, some had long noses and gaping mouths, and one was a skeleton with wings. The naked woman stood in the middle and they were staring at her, ready to prey upon her.

Some had nice strong bodies, they looked awfully well-built to Pete, and their muscles rippled under red satin. She wore a peacock plume for a headdress. She was naked, running suspended, one foot suddenly immobile. Pete felt himself getting hard. His mother came into the room, and Pete slammed the encyclopedia shut. "Your grandmother may be coming to stay the weekend."

The weather wasn't any better and the carts were spread about as usual. Pete and Ray flipped a coin to see who would collect them. Today it was Ray. At lunch Pete sat in the back and talked to Weedy who cut meat. Pete was working on a big provolone hero Gladys Morgan made for him. "That looks good," Weedy said. "Pretty tasty." "Know why I say that, kid?" Wham. "No." "Because it don't have no meat in it." Wham. Two chicken legs, big ones, severed from the body. "Sometimes I sure get sick of this. Wait till they start giving their orders. These people, they don't know what they want." That picture kept coming back to Pete fast as waves in a rainbow. Wham. In waves.

Florence ironed her blouse. "James, there's nothing better than doing simple things. Nothing in the world. Your mind doesn't get a chance to wander. First a shirt, then an apron, then a dress, then some linen. No time to wander, James. And if it does . . . even for a moment . . . it only wanders above." She did Michael's things, bibs and overalls. "Bibs that don't come clean as they should," she sang.

Pete watched TV at Robby Martin's house. It was a color TV. The woman's face was blue with green fringe around it. Pete fiddled with the dial. The color was still a little off.

3

Better now. Soon, though, her face got blue again. Pete slammed his fist against the table. "Why in hell did you do that for?" Robby asked. "I don't know." "Well, look out. You'll splinter the wood, then I'll get blamed for it." "Shut up, anyway." "Make me." Pete jumped off the couch and tackled Robby, knocking him to the floor. He pinned him down and pressed on him with all his weight. "Get off — you're killing me!" But Pete rubbed his face into the rug. "Give . . . ?" Robby spluttered. "No . . . I can't get my breath!" Pete didn't realize he could pin Robby that easily. He didn't realize his own strength. Robby's face was bright red and he was struggling in vain. Pete was a foot from the TV screen. She was in front of him and had started to sing. There was a chorus of men behind her in white coats giving those toothy smiles. "Get up — you're killing me . . ." Close-up of her face. Green with blue fringe. Pete felt himself getting hard. He felt for a minute she was under him. Then he realized it was Robby still squirming. Pete rolled off, embarrassed that Robby might have felt him get hard. But Robby didn't say anything. Nothing. He just lay there panting, gut heaving, her picture above his head. Then they cut away to some man talking.

"Happy birthday!" "Happy birthday, son." "Happy birthday, Pete." "Sixteen candles for my child." "For our strong boy, Mama." Ribbons. Sweaters. Butterscotch ice cream. A hunting knife from his father. "Sixteen candles for our big boy." But later in his room, Pete trembled as he fingered the package he had hidden under his mattress — the only birthday present he really wanted. And he had given it to himself. He had sent away six weeks ago using one of those order blanks from the back page of a comic book. He had bitten his nails past his skin in those weeks, waiting. Finally, his grand-mother had answered the door on a rainy afternoon to find the postman holding the carefully wrapped parcel. She paid the C.O.D. charges, dried off the package and left it in his room. He had saved this moment for when he was in his bed-room alone and everybody else was asleep. He cut the strings with his birthday knife. There they were. His new masks. Remarkably lifelike, supple. Six of them. Sylvester Stallone, Batman, the Creature from the Black Lagoon, a death skull, a wolf salivating, and a laughing fat lady. The last ones were cheapo plastic jobs, and the laughing fat lady looked down-right shabby. He slipped on the Stallone and turned to the mirror. Real lifelike. Covered his whole face. He pictured himself stepping right out of *Rambo*. He even found a comb and pretended to give the slicked-back hair a careless stroke or two. Then he tried the death's-head. Vacant eyes, rotted, corn-colored teeth, and a black widow crawling from the left socket. He hadn't realized he'd unzipped his pants and been jerking off, but now his hand was covered with sperm, some of it was even running along the mirror, and a tiring kind of thrill engulfed him, encouraging him to whisper aloud, "If there were seven steps to hell, I'd take them."

Florence tapped the table. "She's a Godsend, that woman." "Who?" She tapped the table again emphatically. "Phyllis Schlafly, James. Look at her picture on the cover of *Christian Family* . . . it doesn't matter if she's married because a woman like that is really the bride of Christ. . . . She exudes . . . well, she simply exudes . . . holiness . . . ness.

5

That sounds sacred, doesn't it, that double s at the end? *Holy* is one sound, but *ness* is another. She and Reverend Falwell are trying to put a stop to this sickness that you, of course, don't know exists." "Yes, I do, Mother. When two people of the same sex love each other. Carol doesn't think there's anything wrong with that." Florence raised her eyebrows. "She doesn't?" she asked in a wondering tone. She did think so much of Carol and wondered if Carol might know something she didn't.

He cut off the head of the chicken and wiped his brow. "Eating meat today, huh, kid?" "Yeah." "Well, I'm gonna swipe me some lime Jell-o — California Jell-o salad, I think it's called. Don't give me away, huh?" "Sure, Weedy." Pete looked out through the two-way mirror at the meat market. He had been told to keep his eyes open for shoplifters during his lunch hour and if he caught one he'd make ten dollars. He hoped that once he might catch a young girl but he hadn't yet. There he was again. That poor boy with dirt on his face and his legs all scarred. He had an expression of a fox, caught and wounded, but who somehow enjoyed being in the trap even though he hurt. His presence upset Pete. He always seemed to hang around the store in the afternoons. Barefoot and usually bleeding. From what, Pete couldn't figure out. The kid couldn't have been more than nine. One day Pete saw him bend over by the Cokes and Pepsis and set his toes on fire. Pete couldn't believe it. Struck a match and lit his toes. When Pete pounded on the glass, the kid blew on his flesh and a little grey puff of smoke came up and the kid ran. He was raving mad, Pete decided.

Florence looked into her baby's eyes. "You're baptized. Praise be God's." Pete shut the encyclopedia. *Ruby Lacy, Ruby Lacy. When you see me next you'll be half crazy.*

She lived at 1485 Wyoming Street in a small wood house with a ton of acorns rotting on the roof. There was a rotting tree next to it from which a family of squirrels had easy access to the roof. Pete knew her father had deserted her mother years ago and that just the two of them shared the house. Her mother worked until five and Ruby usually got home at four after an ice-cream cone with her girlfriends. The house was not on a busy road so there was nobody to see him peeping in the windows. The squirrels kept kicking the nuts off the roof with their back feet. Once when a car passed, he bent over and picked some up. He could hide his face that way. Ruby had gone from her bedroom to the bathroom and Pete took the opportunity to climb in the window. He stood behind her door and put on the Stallone mask. He could hear her flush the toilet and go into the kitchen. The high tinkling of the spoon told him she was making a glass of iced tea. He figured there was no other sound in the world quite like that. Footsteps. She was coming. When she had crossed the room, he kicked the door shut behind her. She turned to see a stranger in a mask holding a knife casually in front of him. The glass of iced tea dropped from her hands. Shattered. She forgot to scream. Her feet were in pain she kept stepping back and forth on the glass. The voice said, "Take your pants off and you won't get hurt. Call for help and you're dead." Ruby pulled down her blue jeans going back and forth on one foot then the other. "Now lie on the bed." The mask

7

looked stern, brows crossed somewhat apprehensively, but there was a look of concern around the eyes. In a minute, he was on top of her, spreading her legs. He pinned her hands behind her and held them with one hand, with the other he beat her. Pete was behind the mask and he felt himself slide into her. He hit her in the face. "Please do anything, just quit hitting me." Once she pried a hand loose and dug him with her fingernails as hard as she could. But Sylvester Stallone's face didn't bleed. No defense.

At home, Pete put the mask under the mattress and changed clothes. He took a shower. He felt he never wanted to do that again at the same time wanting to do it all over again. He knew no one had seen him. He was a quick jogger. People saw him run home every day after school.

Ruby didn't come back to class until November. Pete was never more excited than on the day she returned. Her face was still bruised, but what was worse, she could hardly move without crutches, her feet swathed in heavy bandages. The cuts. He couldn't resist going up to her between classes. "Ruby, what in the world happened to you?" She answered with a restless look in her eye. "I was in a car accident." "Oh," Pete sympathized. "Not too bad, I hope." She paused. "Oh, no, it looks worse than it is." Pete knew there had been a couple of other "car accidents" since Ruby's and that he had been responsible. He wondered why they hadn't admitted what had happened. Soon the fact that they kept it a secret made him angry. He wanted to put a hole into somebody so deep it would burn right through their clothes.

Wham. "Today your sandwich makes me puke," Weedy

said. Even though school was back in full swing, Pete managed to keep his job part time. Though he regretted the cold days, he never regretted the extra money.

There was only a thin layer of frost on the yard and it wasn't cold so Pete thought nothing of sitting there after dinner. James came up behind him acting like it was the craziest stunt he could imagine. "What do you think we have heaters for, anyway?" "When I get cold, I'll come in." James sat down on the steps. "Gee, you can even see your breath." Pete just wished he would leave him alone. "Pete, did you know I was accepted at college for the fall?" "No . . . that's wonderful." "Well, you see, I'm the first one in my family to go. I am proud about it. Now Carol and I can go together." James looked into Pete's eyes. "Pete . . ." "Yeah?" "Well . . . I hope you don't think I'm trying to be nosy . . . but . . ." Pete suddenly got very cold and he shivered. He shifted weight. "What do you want to say to me, James?" He was surprised to hear his voice shake. "How are your grades this semester, any better?" Pete let out his breath. "Yeah, much better." "That's good, because you want to go to college like me, don't you?" "Yeah, I do." "That makes me happy. Mom and Dad weren't too sure about it, whether you wanted to go or not, but we all want you to go to a good college with values, good moral, no, I don't mean to say that, but someplace that isn't, you know, I don't know . . ." "It's not for another year, anyway." "But we have to think ahead and keep our grades up."

It was the first time her parents had been away the whole year. They had gone up north to see her mother's sick sister. They planned to be back by Tuesday. She couldn't go with them because of student teaching. James drove Carol home. Pete could see him take her up to the door. Her figure shone in the headlights. The garage smelled like spilled milk instead of oil. He wiped his shoes against the wood to be sure they weren't sticky. She let herself in and then James drove away. Pete slipped on his mask. He'd chosen the wolf; he liked it best at night because it was so scary. It even scared him sometimes, it was so ugly. Carol sat at the dining room table, grading papers. Pete figured his paper was with the rest. He crawled in her bedroom window then crouched in the hall. When she got up to go to the kitchen, he sprang at her full force. Her face was so full of terror that for a moment she looked a hundred years old. Pete slugged her in the stomach to knock the wind out of her so she couldn't cry out, then he yanked the floor lamp and threw it in the kitchen. Darkness. He lifted her up then dropped her on top of the table. Her back hit the wood with a deep thud. Then he raped her. When he left he figured she must be hurt because she hardly moved. Back home he looked at the mask. It was fearsome. Carol never talked much about that night. As far as he knew, she never told James the truth. She had slipped and fallen and broken her back and had to be in traction for eight months.

Pete worked late sometimes. Mr. Raney had the choice of either Ray or Pete and he always picked Pete. Pete didn't mind. He enjoyed the night work, stocking shelves, etc. He was now arranging the tomato pastes. Suddenly the lights in the store went out. One by one. It was eerie. Pete looked up. There in the booth sat Mr. Raney, the only light in the place on his desk. He motioned for Pete to come in. Pete took off his apron and slowly made his way. There was something about Mr. Raney today. He coughed for no reason. He avoided Pete when usually he was on his back. His face was lighter than a ghost's. "Close the door behind you . . . like a good boy." Pete felt funny. "Come close . . . . : . Pete." Pete stood right in the light. Raney sat behind him in his swivel chair, his account book on the desk. "I'm going over my business, Pete . . . It's been a profitable year. People will pay anything for food, you know. That's one thing they can't do without." Raney chuckled and Pete didn't like the sound. "Come here." "I can't come any closer, Mr. Raney, or I'd be sitting on your lap." That chuckle again. "But, my boy, that's what I want you to do . . . sit . . ." Raney spread his legs and put his arms around Pete's waist and gently eased him down. Pete squirmed. He hated it. Raney was twice his size. He felt trapped, he wasn't used to feeling this way. "Pete . . ." he whispered, "I'm glad you came to Daddy." The light showed a small hole in Raney's pants. Pete couldn't help staring. "Oh, that?" said Raney. "My wife did it. She's a good woman, Pete, a wonderful wife. But she dropped her cigarette as she was ironing 'em. You know what she did then? She broke into tears and said, 'Oh, God, we don't have any little boy, Homer, we don't have any!' And I cried with her and I told her, 'Honey, there's this boy at my store . . . I think of him as a son.' I do. I do, Pete. Yeah, you're my son. I always wanted a son . . ." Tears swelled. "To do all the things boys like to do . . . play baseball . . . learn to hunt . . . ride a bike . . . play football . . . basketball . . ." His voice cracked. "The things everybody else does but me!" Pete got up. "Do you think you would like to come by, Pete, just say one night a week, one night a week to start, that is, and have dinner with me and my wife?" Pete was out the door. Raney screamed and pounded the desk, tears falling from his face, "I want to go fishing, damn it!"

The laughing fat lady. Pete pulled it from his back pocket. He was so full of hatred for Raney that he knew he could do what he didn't want to do. He thought Mrs. Raney was uglier than sin, but he could pretend she was somebody else. He stood by the bushes, fiddling with the mask. He finally tightened it around his face. Then he saw her. Mrs. Raney. Sitting at the window staring at him. Impossible. He thought he had heard her in the back. But no. She was right at the window sitting as if she hadn't moved all day. She was looking at him with mild curiosity. Pete realized she knew who he was. After all, she must have seen his face. He ripped off the mask and bolted away. He ran home faster than he had ever run before. He collided with his father in the middle of the front yard. "Hey . . ." Rich Grady's deep voice. He cupped Pete on the shoulder. "You go way too fast." Pete gasped. The police must be after him. There was wild fear in his face but Rich didn't seem to notice. Pete ran to his room and hid the mask. He fell on his bed and prayed to God that he wouldn't be caught. Soon he was able to breathe again yet he kept thinking, *She saw me, she saw me.* Time passed and no police came. The only voice was Florence's as she gibbered with the baby. Then she called him to dinner. *Wait a minute,* he thought. *She probably doesn't know about the other girls . . . she might have thought I was some kid . . . with a mask. Yeah, just some kid with a mask.* And he hoped against hope that he was right.

Florence went to the beauty parlor only once a year. The day of the annual picnic. "So early in the spring," she sang as she left the shop. They had done a beautiful job. She looked so presentable. The little brook by the church glowed crisply in the sunlight. Reverend Orry embraced her. "You look wonderful. And not even a sweater." "Oh, no, Reverend. Not on such a Godlike day!" "How right you are." The boys were playing along the brook. "Precious." "More than precious," he corrected her. "Human. Human, but they breathe the breath of God." Florence smoothed her dress. It was a floral print. She looked at the trees. Apple blossoms. Shed by the hundreds. "The smell of spring." "Yes, Florence, it is indeed the smell of spring." The boys ran along the water's edge. "Florence . . . what ideas as a Christian can you offer to see these boys go with God?" Florence thought. "Well, we really can't be happy or at peace without a solid foundation at home, can we, Reverend?" "Indeed not, child." "And I think what concerns most Christian mothers is the breakdown of family life. I think the issue of homosexuality is important when our children are at stake. I certainly want to keep them away from my boys, Pete and James. And those boys out there, I want to keep them away!" "We must. But Florence, you are a good wife and mother. As a woman, you don't have to look so far." "I don't understand, Reverend." "Have you noticed that women seem to have lost their sense of certainty in this age? They say they want more rights, even though they already can kill their own babies. How dare they bring the curse of degradation upon us with these so-called rights? A woman in this town, excuse me for being outspoken, wrote the newspaper that she saw no problem with women sharing public toilets with men." "I can't believe it, nor do I understand it." "Can you think for a minute, Florence, can you think what that means?" Florence was puzzled. "You mean . . . ?" "Just think, that's all, just think." There was an excited shout from the boys. Florence and Reverend Orry saw that they had just hit a frog with a big stone exactly on target. They walked on. "The bells in the church sound musical, Reverend. Very musical. Each time I hear them, I remember to feed the baby. And I think, *His little ears are hearing this, too*. Isn't that a funny thought?" "Yes, but it's thoughts like that coming and going that sometime lead us to a profound discovery . . . something we had no idea was important at the time. You know, I'm now reminded of someone very dear to me who has gone to her reward. Rose Hart, an old-time evangelist, used to come to these spring picnics year after year, and she'd go around and ask everybody, 'Have you ever had a message from The Other World?' And one day I said, 'Yes, Sister, I have,' for I finally saw what she meant." The evening air was warm yet there was something bracing about it. Florence hurried along the sidewalk. She was in such a good mood she was almost skipping. She laughed to herself once, just as the sun slid over the roofs of the parked cars. She had been thinking, *What would Jesus think if He came back to earth today? He would most likely be horrified. And He would be confused about the sharing of the toilets because He wouldn't know what they were used for since they didn't have them in his time!* Florence hugged herself. *Yes, I'll have to teach Jesus about the toilets.* She stepped off the curb into the path of a Honda Accord. The driver tried to brake but it was all so sudden. She was killed instantly, that was a mercy to the family. The driver felt so badly he came to the funeral. He explained to Pete and James and to Rich, "God forgive me, there was nothing I could do." The lid came down on the coffin. Pete crossed himself as they laid his mother in the grave.

Several nights later the men ate a lonely dinner. Finally Rich Grady broke the silence and in his usual stern, unquavering voice, he said, "Listen. I want you boys to understand this. This house still has a sense of order, a sense of decency. Your mother and I discussed if something like this ever happened — you were not to think of her anymore as Florence. She wants you to think of her as Mary. You understand?" Pete wondered why the lights were turned off in the living and dining rooms while they ate. The light in the kitchen lit the table indirectly. Harshly. The next night he flipped on the other lights and no one took exception so he guessed everybody had just forgotten. Pete learned to change Michael's diapers. He didn't like the job but his father insisted. One night the baby screamed bloody murder. Pete thought then of raping somebody.

On Friday he came home from school, threw his books on his desk and flopped onto the bed. He put his hands under the mattress to pull out The Creature from the Black Lagoon. His fingers only felt the springs. Desperately he pushed his hands further under. Nothing. He leaped off the bed and pulled the mattress up. Gone. All of them. Who had found them? His father? Brother? Pete was in shock. He broke into a cold sweat. He fell in front of the mirror and prayed that everything would be all right. Then he told his father he had a stomachache, which was true, and got into bed for the night. He woke in the dark from a terrible dream. He found he was crying. He never never wanted to have that dream again. He had heard something in the basement. "Who's there?" No answer. He turned on the flashlight and walked slowly from his room. He walked and walked for hours, past all familiar objects in his house, but now he lingered over each one with microscopic eyes even though he was moving all the time. Gliding, shuddering, knowing what he would find when he opened the door. Finally that moment came. The bright beam of the flashlight. The door springing back. From the depths of the basement wandered that poor boy from the store, a hunk of concrete torn out of the wall where he had been chained. His arm was still tightly bound and little worms of blood popped around the metal. He came up the stairs, plaster and blood in his hair, a cruel, defiant smile on his lips. He was grateful to Pete for rescuing him . . . but even more grateful to Pete for having chained him. Pete woke with a cry. The dream faded.

The next morning brought the sun and with it a new strength. The cobwebs and tired old spiders were brushed away along with the moon and stars. Pete thought of a girl and her eleven-year-old sister who lived near the woods. They never took the bus. They had a leisurely country breakfast and then walked to school. He thought of grabbing them from behind a tree before they had a chance to rub the sleep from their eyes. He looked down the hall. The door to his mother's room was open. He had not been inside since she died. Now he went without a thought to her drawer and pulled out one of her old stockings. This would make an ideal mask. Simple. It would distort his features and probably not be so hot. Inexpensive as well.

Graduation Day found Pete in a coat and tie. His hand played with the stocking in his coat pocket. His fingers massaged the nylon. He listened to the seniors give their good-bye speeches. *Good-bye, Good-bye*, thought Pete. It was sunny so the Principal had set up chairs outside. James sat proudly on the stage. And when he was called forward and handed his diploma he smiled at the audience but singled out Pete in particular. Pete looked up at the sky. There was a moon in a blue sky — Pete had seen it before in the daytime, but he couldn't remember if he was really looking at the moon or its reflection. James began his speech. Pete grudgingly admitted it sounded better than the principal's. Something about a visionary stance of the world. But he imagined it was only one of many to come, there were nine other students waiting on the stage. He sighed and tried to block it out. He looked back up in the sky. The sun and moon collided. This omen told him nothing new. Survival of the fittest.

NAMELESS THING

IT WAS A BLACK TRIANGULAR ROOM AND IT HAD A MIRROR IN it. A full mirror rounded at the top glued onto the front of a cedar closet. His bed was in the corner and the mirror was turned slightly away from his line of vision so that he never once saw himself — only a section of the room . . . empty, angled, distorted.

He thought of it now because he was standing at a funny angle looking into the men's room mirror and not seeing himself but another man down the way whom he hadn't even known was in the room. A short, middle-aged man adjusting his tie with a faded design of candied grapes and cherries running down a black stripe. The man had a shock of red hair and a thin neck and a face that reminded him of a reptile. A sickly grin from rubbery lips. An ugly parrot in an ill-kept cage.

Georgi was cold and he felt alone, more than he had ever felt before. He lit a cigarette and thought of how people watched you all the time and you didn't even know it. He walked outside to the rest area. Trucks were pulling in for the night. Bright headlights bore down on him and he had to jump to miss a collision with the fenders.

Bastard, Georgi swore.

The trucker leaned out his window and was about to offer a mean retort, but did a double take of Georgi, then made a disgusted motion with his hand as if to say forget it and drove on. Sure, he's tired and exhausted, Georgi thought. Probably frustrated as hell about his job or wife or something secret. Truckers have lots of secrets, probably. More than men in other professions. They're dirty, too. Georgi had seen all the graffiti in the toilets. So what. So what to all of it, Georgi thought bitterly. It's other things he wondered about . . . other secrets . . .

He walked along the edge of the rest stop. A string of cars was parked in the dark. He could see motionless shadows at the wheels though how they could rest with the constant noise of heavy, dusty motors bearing down at 90 m.p.h. on the highway a mere body's length away, he didn't know. It was hard for him to sleep. He made his way down the line of cars, careful not to get too close like he had that first night when he approached a woman for a ride. She had cried out. So he didn't ask at night anymore.

There was a row of trees along the side beyond which was an empty plain. Two trees grew together. It was here he had constructed a hammock with a cheap Mexican blanket and some chicken wire. It was twelve feet off the ground because at that point the trees bent close together and provided enough space to stretch the blanket across. So he had to shimmy up the tree, test the wire to be sure it was holding up, then roll onto the blanket. No snakes up here, nor scorpions. Nothing but the noise to prevent him from a good, soothing sleep.

Dawn came early and brought a frost. Georgi shivered in the blanket. There was something bearable, though, about a

Texas winter morning because within a couple of hours it would turn pleasant. He opened an eye and caught the white sky full of light clouds being born and beginning to drift slowly towards him on a straight, chilly path.

At noon, he dropped down the side of the tree to find two teenaged girls in the midst of a picnic lunch at one of the wooden tables. They were trying to protect their peanut butter and jelly sandwiches from a zealous bee. Georgi danced over to them and while the girls watched silently, their mouths dropping, he deftly whisked the bee into his hand. Then, as if performing a feat of magic, he danced around a little rock, picked it up, lay the bee in an air pocket and replaced the rock on top of it. He then finished his impromptu jig and bowed. One of the girls applauded, but the other stared blankly, unsure of her emotions.

"Thank you," the applauding girl laughed.

"You are most welcome," Georgi answered graciously.

There was a moment of uncomfortable silence and then the girls went back to their lunch.

But Georgi was not put off and he zeroed in on them.

"Why, you just come up to the table top," the girl observed wistfully.

"Yes, of course. I'm a dwarf. My name's Georgi."

"Hello. I'm Leigh, that's Jody." She pointed across the table to a girl with red hair who purposely ignored them. Georgi had met her type before, but she wouldn't get the best of him. But he would have to work through Leigh.

"You girls haven't by chance seen the circus, have you?"

"You mean the one that's outside El Paso? No, do you work

there?"

"Yes, I do. I'm a clown, a dancing clown." He was not one of the dancing clowns, but the girls would never know it.

"You've been meaning to take your little brother there, haven't you, Jody?"

"I suppose," Jody mumbled. "We should be going soon, Leigh. Finish your lunch."

"Yes," Leigh sighed. "We have a very long drive ahead of us."

Georgi pursed his lips into a smile and asked, "And where are you going, might I ask?"

"Well, we — " But Jody kicked her under the table and Leigh held her breath. Then she glared at Jody and blurted, "We're going to Denver!"

"Beautiful. Colorado, huh?"

Leigh nodded and crumbled the brown wax paper stained with peanut butter.

"I'll take it for you," Georgi offered.

"Will you? That's nice of you." She handed him the wrapper and she and Jody got up.

"Girls," Georgi said seriously. "Girls . . . would you give me a lift . . . not as far as Colorado, but anywhere out of here. I'm all alone and . . ."

"It's out of the question," Jody's voice shook. "Completely out of the question."

After the girls had made a hasty departure, Georgi lifted the rock. There was the bee, its wings brushed by sunlight. Georgi smothered it in a glob of peanut butter then placed the rock on top of bee and wrapper. He said aloud, "Bee stings are bad and painful things." He sat on top of the rock and burst into tears.

Later that day, he tried others, but they offered him no escape. He made his pleas more and more urgent, but the harder he tried, the quicker he failed. A young couple lied and insisted they had no extra room in their camper, a truck driver laughed at him, and an elderly man threatened to phone the police.

The sun was his enemy. When it sank, he knew his attempts to find a ride were over for the day. He headed into the men's room and washed his hands, asked a stranger to press the hot air button for him, then stood under the dryer, lifting his hands above his head and closing his eyes to keep the dust and lint out.

He climbed the tree and crawled into the hammock. The night brought sounds of car doors opening, slamming shut, opening again. A constant trail of people coming and going. He must find a way out. He thought of the way he had come here. Then further back still to when the circus had first put stakes into the ground on the shiny plateau outside El Paso. He suddenly was back there, sitting with her . . .

The first sunny morning in spring found Hilda secluded in her trailer sewing sequins on the air balls the clowns used to balance on their heads and then toss to the seals.

Elb called to her. "Hilda, what in the name of the Beloved Christ are you doing in there in the dark? It's the first day it ain't been clouded over for a week. Come on outside."

"There's too much work to do," the voice flowed through the window.

"For the love of God you can pull your chair outside and sew in the sun."

"I can't because the sequins lose their sparkle in the light and I won't be able to see what I'm sewing."

"Have it your way."

Hilda bounced the ball a few times. "There, that one is finished." She smiled over at Georgi who sat complacently across from her, building a house of cards. "You never finished telling me where you come from."

Georgi coughed. "Well, I don't know exactly."

"You don't have no American accent . . . and it ain't Mexican either." She ran a silver thread through a gap in her teeth and it came out wet and gray. "You're from Italy, huh? A family of circus folks?"

"No," Georgi hedged. "I ain't from a circus family, Hilda."

"Then how did you come to work in this place?"

Georgi felt like reminding her that the "work" he did was nothing more than emptying pails of animal slop into woods or into creeks at every town they played. Slop from tigers, elephants, and seals. He only said, "I ain't a performer, Hilda."

Hilda said quickly, "No, of course you ain't." She hoped she hadn't hurt his feelings. "No, you don't have to squeeze into ugly suits and get out in front of hundreds of folk while they gawk at you. I'm no performer either. We know the ropes, huh, Georgi?"

Hilda was in charge of the costumes and props. This had given her ample opportunity to meet and become friendly with everybody in the troupe. They had scheduled fittings before each show and Hilda's hands were never at rest as there was always a costume crisis to attend to, no matter the hour or circumstance.

Everybody liked Hilda, Georgi reasoned. He guessed though he liked her about best of all. She had the most beautiful face of anybody he ever saw, like an angel. It was warm and blonde and her hair hung to her shoulders. Some called her fat and he supposed she was, but a stunning kind of fat, the kind that flattered, the kind that was never meant to be exchanged for a drab, slimmer self. She wore light dresses that clung to her no matter what the season and her cleavage was always showing. Georgi was in awe of her breasts, just like all the other men. He was sometimes apt to fantasize, picturing the breasts heaving behind flimsy material with a life of their own separate from her. But then he would be suddenly struck by her warmth and would look at her breasts but couldn't see them. Her breath was her own again.

No one knew where she came from. Some guessed her to be from Germany because of her appearance and lingering accent. But the clown master insisted she was "a sturdy Viking from Norway" while the manager of the circus referred to her as a Greek.

"You never did tell me," she continued, bouncing another ball with assurance and aplomb, "what kind of family you come from."

"No kind. They drunk themselves to death in a New York gutter, I guess when they saw what kind of son they birthed."

"Lies. You can't tell me they was that way and had a son that turned out nice as you."

Georgi considered a moment, then admitted, "No, they was OK kinds of folk. They liked me good enough, Hilda. I just made that other up."

"Of course you did. I can sure tell, hearing everybody's story in here like I do, what's made up and what ain't. I have a sixth sense. It is six, ain't it, or seven?"

"I don't know."

"Well, there's the sense of touch, sight, smell, taste . . ." Her voice trailed off mysteriously. "Ain't there another one? I always list them in a different order and always leave a different one out each time."

Georgi added the last fragile card to the top of his house.

Hilda chuckled and winked at him. "That's a nice house. You used all hearts that time. I like it, your house of hearts."

At dinner in the big tent, Georgi paused slightly to nod to Hilda. Elb Grew had managed to get a seat next to her and he scowled as Georgi passed by with his slop bucket. Georgi overheard Elb say, "I saw him comin' out of your trailer this afternoon. What do you spend so much time on him for?"

"He's a nice person."

"Yeah, well you can't get friendly with everybody, 'specially not a midget."

Georgi headed towards the cages, hot under the collar. He hated that man for talking the way he did. Elb Grew was always on his back about something. He was a tall man around forty and Georgi always sensed that Grew loved to menace him with his towering figure. One time he almost stood on his foot while he made some comment about the weather. Accidentally on purpose, Georgi had decided.

The seals were whining in the cages, nudging lackadaisically one of Hilda's new sequined bouncing balls.

During summer, attendance increased and there was a heavy demand in Texas for greasepaint, acrobatics, and glossy, black ponies to carry babies around and around the ring. The troupe worked hard and pushed themselves to the point of expiration on Saturdays and Sundays. Monday was the day off.

Elb knocked on Hilda's trailer. "How about you and me takin' a nice ride to the river. It's a beautiful day."

"Why that would be wonderful, only . . ."

"Only what?" Elb muttered anticipating her answer.

"Well, that we can take Georgi along, too."

"Damn it — "

"Oh, wait a minute, Elb. Taking him along don't matter a whit. That don't mean nothin'."

"Third wheel, he'll be a third wheel."

"All right, let him be a third wheel. He never goes anywhere."

Georgi and Hilda had become inseperable companions during the last few weeks. He would visit her in the evenings and she soon had him helping her with the fittings.

After coffee, he would climb outside and sleep under her trailer since the circus provided no accomodations for him.

Elb drove them in his powerhouse truck which he used during the week to move the tents and circus props. Elb was in charge of the transportation, and three other men reported directly to him. He enjoyed a cigar as he caressed the wheel with his free hand. Hilda sat next to him while Georgi leaned against the passenger door.

"When did you take up cigars, it's a foul habit. If you don't throw it out, I will have to take Georgi on my lap."

Elb blew some bulky smoke rings in her face, tossed the stub out the window, and leaned back and howled while he listened to her angry reprimands. "It's all right, I'm hungry, anyway. Don't want my smoke to spoil my meal."

They pulled in at Col. Sanders Kentucky Fried Chicken and Georgi went up to get two buckets of chicken, slaw, rolls, and potatoes. When Hilda saw him struggling with the load of food, she made a move to help him but Elb held her back, "Let the midget do his share."

The three were so hungry they had finished their meal by the time they parked at the scenic river. They heard it before they saw it, a turbulent rush of water clashing stubbornly with the very canyon walls that contained it. This was no example of the peaceful coexistence of the forces of nature.

The wind lashed at them, cutting along their cheeks.

"Don't stand too close to the edge, it's too windy!" Elb warned.

Hilda stumbled backward with a feeble cry. "I had no idea."

"Sure," Elb continued. "Hypnotizes you, that river, when you look down at its dark blue stream. Then you don't notice things like the wind. It's only up close, you don't feel it a few feet away. One night, Jess Cole and me were drinkin' up here and he got too near that rim right there and the wind gave him a tumble and I'll be damned if I didn't have to give him a hand to stop him from spillin' right over the edge." He laughed. "It's sure hot here with the sun on you. There ain't no bigger sight in the world, not for my money, than the Rio Grande!"

Hilda stared dreamily across the gorge to Mexico. "Ever been across there, Georgi?"

"No."

"Me neither," she said. "Sure is pretty, though. Look at that land, it just stretches on and on. Lord, and that clear blue sky over it. Makes me shudder."

Elb, taking advantage of her moment of awe, slipped his arm quietly around her waist. "I been down there. Lots of times. When I was nineteen or so, I visited all them places. Juarez, Zaragoza, rode the cutest damn mule you ever saw."

"A mule? It didn't try to fight you off?" Hilda wondered.

"No . . . you wouldn't fight me off, either, would you, if I climbed onto you?"

"Oh, yes, I would."

He tightened his grip.

"Why'd you go there, anyway?" she asked, her voice cracking.

"My buddy and I were havin' the times of our lives, looking for platinum and precious metals. There was a rush of rumors around that time that there was a gold streak along near Bravos. We made it there and it looked just like that land across the river, and we went on and there was nothin' but beautiful earth all the way from Bravos south to El Povenir."

"Of course, you never did come across any precious metals," Hilda teased.

Elb became strangely serious and looked into her eyes. "No, Hilda, I didn't." But she had the uncomfortable feeling he was talking about something else.

Georgi was angry with himself for having come along at Hilda's insistence since he could never be himself with Elb around to hound him. He should have stayed at the circus and tried to show Moose Farrell that he was a hard worker in the hopes of getting a better job. He kicked a stone over the canyon wall but, of course, could neither see nor hear it once it started its fall. He did hear laughter from behind the truck, where Elb had cornered Hilda and was making swooping noises as if he were a giant eagle excited at the prospect of kissing its prey. Only the prey was resisting.

Later, Hilda tried to comfort him in her own way. "Are you thirsty?" she asked him.

"Yes," he said.

"Can I get a drink for you in a cup from that fountain? It's awful high."

"I can reach it." Georgi was determined to reach the spout, under the watchful gaze of Hilda and Elb, even though it hurt every inch of his body and stretched every muscle, even though his eyes closed with the pain. He held on to finally feel the cold jet of water splash his face.

Hilda latched the door behind the new bareback rider and watched her disappear into the dark. She turned to Georgi who sat at the table under her red lamp building card houses.

"Where do you think she came from?" Hilda asked.

Georgi shrugged as Hilda sat back down and began to sew the rhinestones on the bareback rider's blue costume.

"I think she's illegal . . . from across the border. Did you notice she never said a word to me when I was fitting her? That means she don't speak a word of English. Of course, I don't care. It's Moose's business who he hires." She paused and watched Georgi intent on his card house and tonight using the entire deck, not just one suit. He had stacked spade upon club, heart upon diamond, and was now trying to carefully place the four queens on top of the rest. "You know, Georgi," Hilda continued. "I don't care who Moose hires and I told him so. As long as he treats the rest of us OK."

"I did it," Georgi muttered as the fifty-second card found its upright place in the house.

"Tomorrow morning, you begin work as a seal trainer."

Georgi looked up through the red light to Hilda. He frowned a moment then slowly began taking the house apart card by card. "I don't understand," he said slowly.

"It's simple, I fixed it up with Moose. Told him you was OK and a good worker. You should be given a chance to do something besides . . . well, what you do."

"That's so good of you." Georgi began to tremble and tears came to his eyes.

"All right now, stop it," she said. "No scenes and that is that." She stood up and opened her closet which was jammed with costumes of all kinds. She kneeled and pulled a hat box from the closet floor and set it on his lap.

"Open it," she said.

Georgi pulled off the lid and found a little ringmaster's costume, an elegant little coat and tails outfit with pearl buttons.

"I'll help you into it," Hilda said and began to undress Georgi. He was embarrassed to show her his chest but when he caught a glimpse of it in the mirror he realized it wasn't bad at all and thrust it out proudly towards her. When she finally fitted him, Georgi felt as if he didn't know himself.

"I'll never forget this, Hilda," Georgi said. "Never forget what you've done for me."

Hilda shook her head. "What better things do I have to do with my time? I have no one." She sat back down and once again her face was colored red. "No one." She picked up the nine of diamonds, then found the eight, then the seven. She scrutinized them carefully, then stacked them in a pile. "Your card houses. You live in them, Georgi, don't you? That's where you live. I understand that and I think it's wonderful. I wish I could live in one, too."

Georgi put the deck of cards in his pocket.

"My aunt is a very old woman back in Hungary," Hilda said, her eyes getting bigger. "I haven't seen her for ten years. Maybe she's dead. But I don't think so. She comes from a family of survivors. And one day I'll go back and claim her. Gypsies. That's what they are. They've lived their lives in storms, violent, no end to them. Ain't it wild? When a rainstorm hits these prairies, I think of them. Always hiding. When soldiers came and I was a little girl we each had our own tree and we'd step behind it and they never saw us. They weren't shit to us. We lived in the forest and used the big

34

trees like blankets. Soldiers weren't shit to us. We lived by spells . . . by magic . . ."

"No, there is no way I would do it. Ever!"

"For God's sake, have pity on him. He ain't got no place to go. Put him in your trailer!"

"I can't."

"Why not?"

"Dammit, I'd feel like there was somebody watchin' me all the time, that's why."

"Your imagination — "

"That slop carrier — "

"He don't do that no more and you know it. His job is as respectable as yours. And he signed a two year contract with Moose Farrell and I watched him put his big X right on the paper and it was a thrillin' moment for him and me!" Hilda stopped, out of breath. Elb glared at her and threw open the back of his truck.

"Here's all the space I got," he said.

Hilda walked into the truck filled with props, mirrors, an old bed, black curtains. She motioned for Elb to follow her. He groaned and hoisted himself up and sat on the bed.

"There's more than enough room. Look at them two big sideboards. Tack 'em up and block off that space for him." Hilda showed him how with hand movements.

"Oh, Christ," he sighed. "I don't want to live with a midget."

Hilda stared a hole through him. "I know you," she snorted. "You're no good. What is it you want, my tits or my ass?"

Elb Grew spit towards her, then waved his arm in exasperation. "I'm tired of fighting you."

"Well, good. Then you can build a little room for him.
Here, put up those boards so they come together in a point.
I'll have a dresser brought over, the one Moose's wife ain't
usin' with the mirror on it, you can drape those black curtains
over the wall, and then you can have the whole rest of the
truck to yourself."

"Gee, thanks," Elb said. "One other thing, I know you're
gonna show me them tits and ass sometime soon."

Georgi was comfortable in Elb's truck even if Elb would-
n't speak to him. The room was just the right size for him and
by his bed there was a little table with a drawer where he
could keep his cards. For every show he would spend at least
an hour dressing until he, himself, was shocked by his sense
of perfection. Then he would stride into the ring.

By winter he had a good sense of control over the four
seals and was skilled at making them do tricks. He used a
little riding crop on them, to get them to bounce the ball
or jump through the hoop, but he barely touched them with
it. Though he performed at the same time the bareback
girls were lying sidesaddle across the palominos and at the
same time the trapeze artist was making his entrance, he
nonetheless felt that he had taken center stage and that the
audience was completely with him. Once he had looked up
and seen Hilda smiling and waving with encouragement and
he had never felt happier. Afterwards, Hilda had knelt and
kissed him.

That night he opened the truck to find Grew lounging on

his bed.

"What are you doing here?" Georgi asked.

Elb indolently lit a cigar and dropped the match on the floor. "What am I doing here? It's my truck, ain't it?"

"Of course."

"And it seems to me like I have a right to be here when I please." Georgi took off his hat and placed it on the table. He began to unlace his shoes, becoming more and more intimidated by Grew's presence but trying not to show it by giving full concentration to the mechanical process of undressing.

"This place is becomming a bit 'untidy,'" Grew added.

"I'm sorry you think so . . ."

"Try to keep it up, it's the least you can do."

Georgi flushed a deep red since both he and Grew knew he kept the place spotless. He couldn't help blurting out, "You can take your muddy feet off the bed for starts."

"What did you say," Grew reached out and grabbed Georgi and pulled him over to the bed.

"You heard me."

Grew didn't relax his grip on the dwarf. "Why, I ought to put my cigar out in your pretty little face."

Georgi pushed back with all his strength. "Let go."

"Shut up." Grew pressed hard on his spine.

"Let go of me!"

"Quit squeakin', I tell ya!"

Georgi finally pulled away and tumbled onto the floor. "I'm not squeakin'."

"Sure, you're squeakin' you miserable little . . . you don't talk, you squeak!" Grew stood up and leaned over Georgi, his hands on his hips. Georgi wiped a little blood off his mouth. Grew's eyes narrowed. "How do you like it, standin' in a big man's shadow." Georgi fixed his eyes straight ahead on Grew's knees. "Well, I don't like it, you hear? Why are you always around her? Why are you always botherin' Hilda? Why do you always follow her like a sick dog?"

"I don't."

"Oh, yes, you do. I've seen it. You like to see them two melons of hers hanging over the table. I know."

"No."

"Well, I'm telling you this. You got a contract here and you gotta stay, but you don't have to go around her. If you ever do again, or go into her trailer I'll see to it you don't work the tent again!"

Georgi was afraid of Grew but felt that his threat was hollow because he was too big a coward to jeopardize his own job by causing trouble over at the tent in trying to get him fired. But he didn't want any further ugly confrontations so he did stay away from Hilda. At least he stopped going around her trailer at night.

"What's wrong, Georgi, don't you want to come see me, anymore?" she asked him one night at dinner.

Georgi cast his eyes to his plate of corn and Spanish rice. "Yeah, but I need plenty of sleep. For my job."

"Of course you do."

Georgi found that the minute he was denied access to Hilda, she was all that he could think about. He kept seeing her everywhere and hearing her voice. She was in his dreams and would linger long in his mind after he woke up. Try as he would, he couldn't stop dwelling on her.

One day a group of merchants from downtown El Paso drove out to the circus in a gleaming station wagon filled with boxes of knickknacks to peddle to the performers. Georgi made some money now so he could afford the present for Hilda. He paid the man three dollars.

That night he wrapped it in a handkerchief. He waited until he heard Elb Grew snoring, then he quietly slipped out the back of the truck. He crept to Hilda's trailer and called to her softly. There was no answer. Georgi decided to try again a little louder but broke into an ugly sweat at the thought that Grew, not Hilda, would be the one to hear his whispers. But soon he heard the latch pull back and she peered out into the dusty, cool night. She was wearing a long white nightgown made of a kind of see-through gauze.

"Come in," she smiled.

Georgi immediately presented her with the handkerchief.

"For me?" she asked.

His eyes clouded over at the sound of her voice. The sound he had missed for a long time.

She unwrapped the present. With an exclamation she held it up to the light. A beautiful crucifix. With Jesus' face at the center. His eyes and lips punctuated by what seemed like rubies.

"What a gift," she cried. She rubbed the cross against her breasts and held it firmly there. "This shows me I was right about helping and taking you in. This is a blessing."

It was a Monday night but Georgi decided to clean the seals' cage and perhaps practice a new routine or two. The only light he had was from his match and as he lit his cigarette, he stared at one of the seals nudging a ball. Then he was startled by something cold on his neck. He slapped at whatever was behind him and when he turned he saw it was one of the seals towering above him on a rope, hanging by its neck. Georgi looked down. He was standing in a pool of fresh blood. He pushed the seal away from him and his hands got all bloody. Then he realized for the first time that the dead seal was dressed in his ringmaster's outfit.

Georgi backed away in terror, holding his ears to block out the wail of the seals. They seemed to be calling to him, begging him to come back. But he ran as fast as he could, he ran down the shiny plateau away from the circus and never looked back. He ran as fast as he could, he didn't care where. He didn't stop until he fell with exhaustion about a hundred feet from the rest area next to Interstate Highway 10.

Georgi felt himself waking to the bright Texas morning. He opened his eyes and uttered a cry of surprise. There was Hilda, her figure in the white sky, blowing overhead like a large balloon, her light dress flowing. She was tied to a cross and she and the cross tilted down toward the earth and she was inspecting the country below as she drifted by, ignoring the billowy clouds that sometimes moved across her face.

He sat up and rubbed his eyes. Then he climbed down the tree and watched the cars and trucks approach the entrance to the rest stop. Some shot right in, some slowed down with indecision and then swerved away at the last minute.

Georgi felt feverish all day. He didn't act as usual, plotting his escape and choosing the travelers most likely to give him a ride. Instead he stood silently in a barren field as if he were listening for something. Once he muttered something about the "rumbling of wheels" and bent his ears to the ground and nodded his head as if he had heard something significant. Then he mumbled again, "The sense of sound, Hilda. The one you couldn't remember . . . It was the sense of sound . . ." He stood in the field all day muttering to himself.

As evening came, he appeared more frightened. He cast shadowy glances toward the parked cars. His lips were twisted with a steadfast apprehension. "I must move now," he said and hurried to the cars.

Darkness fell. He threw himself on the mercy of an Air Force officer.

"Please," he stomped his feet hysterically on the cement. "I've just told you I've been here for five goddam days and five goddam nights. What do you want to hear from me? What must I give you? See, over there in that tree, that's where I've slept, I tell you — "

The officer literally pushed him away and drove off. Georgi twirled to find the headlights bearing down on him. He threw his hands over his face. The truck stopped short. The motor idled. Elb Grew got out.

"So this is where you've been? We've all been worried sick! Come on."

"I don't want to go back."

"Don't be silly. You have to."

"I'll never go back!"

Grew stammered impatiently, "Moose Farrell told me to bring you back no matter what, you have a contract to live up to, you can't just walk out. You're going back!"

Elb Grew lifted the sobbing man, opened the back of his truck, threw him in and padlocked the door. Then he drove away.

Georgi lay inside dreading his return. How would he face Hilda? Moose? Any of the others? What would they say to him? How would they act? He wished he could sleep but he wasn't tired. He could occasionally hear other trucks pass by and he counted them. He was up to fifteen when they stopped.

Georgi heard Grew get out, but he didn't come for him. Instead he walked somewhere and kicked something. Georgi listened. There was no sound of the circus. There was hardly any sound. Then he heard the wind. And he heard the river rushing below. The steel blue canyons of the Rio Grande. He listened to the wind and the water and his heart stuck in his mouth. He knew exactly where they were. He heard Grew's footsteps approaching. He was coming for him now. Grew's hands pulled on the lock. Georgi opened his eyes wide and looked around him.

It was a black triangular room and it had a mirror in it. A full mirror rounded at the top glued onto the front of a cedar closet. His bed was in the corner and the mirror was turned slightly away from his line of vision so that he never once saw himself — only a section of the room . . . empty, angled, distorted.

RAPHAEL

"WILL YOU WATCH MY SON FOR A MINUTE?" KATHRYN HURST asked breathlessly. "I've just been paged."

The saleswoman, standing at attention behind the glass case of truffles and other confections, sensed the urgency in her tone and briskly nodded.

Kathryn brushed Raphael's blond hair back from his forehead, whispering, "You wait right here for me. Mommy has to go talk to her lawyer." And throwing her mink coat over her shoulders, she executed an abrupt turn and raced across the lobby, her high heels making no sound on the vast Oriental carpet.

Raphael's eyes glided from one truffle to the next, each neatly labeled in flowery handwriting; the woman discreetly directed her gaze elsewhere which left Raphael the freedom to fantasize without embarrassment about the sunshiny orange-chocolate curls and the vanilla Brazils laced with Grand Marnier. Now and then, interrupting his reverie, came a muffled tinkle from the bell captain's quarters and Raphael was reminded that Christmas was only a few days away. Not that he needed another reminder. All day long, guests had been sweeping into the Plaza, snow sitting on their shoulders, the porters in attendance cheerfully struggling under packages they would never see the contents of — gifts from Tiffany's or Cartier's — presents, quickly passing from their arms to those of their owners, whose worth was more than they would possess in a lifetime.

Raphael moved a few feet away to the newsstand and as he scanned with little comprehension the headlines of the world in ten different languages, he became aware of the renewed scrutiny of the saleswoman. He caught her curious stare as she flicked away the imaginary specks of dust that threatened the truffles.

His mother, a holiday whirlwind, was suddenly upon him. "Your daddy evidently will stop at nothing to find out where we are," she announced, half in glee, half in terror. "He's hired the finest private eyes his money can buy. It doesn't surprise me. We just have to be on guard . . . Why, one of them could be sitting right over there in that cluster of leather armchairs, keeping his trained eye on everybody who comes in and out."

But the only people sitting there were a very old couple, each with canes, deep in a slow conversation, and Raphael doubted very much if they were detectives.

"You aren't afraid, are you?" His mother pulled a face sad as the moon.

"No."

"Well, there's some justice then. Come on, honey, let's go upstairs. I'm bushed."

Kathryn soaked in the deep bathtub which was shaped like a shell, its edges fluted pink marble. She had deftly wrapped her hair — blonde like her son's, only thinner — in a heated towel. Though she was in repose, her arms resting languidly over the sides of the tub, her mind was busy trying to banish fearful scenarios — her "what-ifs" and "what-nows" — but they kept spinning free and plaguing her. Raphael was straightening the perfumes on the terra-cotta vanity.

"You know, it's not me your daddy wants to get hold of," she blurted. "It's you. He doesn't care if the divorce goes through and I'm left with five million. He just wants to be sure we aren't together anymore." Raphael massaged the nape of her neck. "Oh, that feels wonderful. So relaxing . . . You don't know how I need to relax." Raphael stared down into the soapy water where his mother's knees looked like two sunbaked desert islands. "We'll go out tonight for a lovely holiday supper. We'll celebrate. We'll stay up late. We'll forget. Would you like that?"

"Very much." His hands continued to rub her flesh.

"He wants you to go to college. One doesn't go to college to be educated these days. One goes to Europe. The pendulum has swung back. One goes to the Rijksmuseum with a sketch pad, to La Scala to hear Verdi or Bellini, one stands in silence in the shadows of Westminster Abbey or Nôtre Dame. We'll leave next week. We'll ring in the New Year on the other side of the ocean."

"But my last term . . ." It wasn't a protest but a declaration of indifference.

"Experience of the world and all its pleasures. That counts for something, I should think. Whatever seizes your fancy along the way — poetry, architecture, painting — we'll pursue. This will be your eighteenth birthday present. It's a bit early since you won't actually turn eighteen until February, but you won't mind, will you?"

"No." Raphael began humming.

"Help me up, sweetheart, I don't want to turn to a mass of wrinkles." Raphael helped his mother out of the bathtub. Though she was in her early forties, she had still kept her slim figure and good looks. "My breasts haven't begun to think about falling," she laughed as she examined herself in the circular, mirrored room. She dabbed a touch of perfume behind each ear. "Get me my glass, will you?"

Raphael found her glass by the bed which was nestled in a black onyx enclosure at one end of the suite. When he returned she was rummaging through her pillbox that contained dozens of pills in as myriad shapes as snowflakes. She gulped down four of them and Raphael pictured them disappearing magically in her throat like snowy crystals. "Now," she began, "you must get into the tub before the water gets cold." She began unbuttoning his shirt. "My," she said with just a splinter of annoyance, "you've become a big boy, a full head taller than I am, and big-boned too."

"Can't be helped."

"No, of course not." She placed his shirt on the dresser then unbuttoned his pants. "Step out of them." Raphael did as instructed. Then, without a pause, she slipped off his underpants and he stood naked before her. "My handsome darling," she beamed. "Do you want me to wash you?"

"No, I just want to sit quietly in the tub."

"All right. Don't be too long." Gathering his clothes under her arm, she moved toward the suite. "Want the door open or shut?"

"Shut."

"Don't slip on the tiles."

"I won't. Don't worry."

With the click of the door, Raphael's shoulders sagged with relief. He approached the tub. The bubbles had spread apart and left a pink film on top of the water. He put his finger into the liquid. Ice cold.

Uncertainly, he sat down on the toilet and stared for some time at his reflection in the mirrors. His creamy white skin and creamier blond hair came back at him so many times, from so many places, that it seemed he was dreaming and he half expected one of the Raphaels to step out of the glass and wake him up. But they were too busy looking pretty to bother.

He thought of the afternoon about a week ago when Peter had picked him up at his private school to drive him back home. Raphael, snuggled under a woolen blanket, had watched his chauffeur with fascination, the black cap and gloves fitting wonderfully on a man who resembled a crafty animal more than a human being. Peter had given him quick glances in the rearview mirror while carefully fingering his dark mustache. Finally, Peter said with real confusion, "You're about as pretty as my girlfriend, you know that?" Raphael had felt faint and his throat too strangled to give a response. Peter turned his attention to the traffic sloshing through the winter weather and Raphael played with the corner of the blanket.

"I don't hear any water splashing," he heard his mother's voice.

"I said I just wanted to sit quietly."

He could hear her bustling around the suite, so he got up noiselessly and locked the door.

His mother's lipsticks were arranged in a neat line on top of the earthenware vanity, and though several Raphaels approached, it was only one who selected the red ice and twisted it till the sloping peak couldn't rise any higher. Trembling slightly, he brought it to his lips. He painted them, making sure he didn't smudge his teeth which shone even whiter behind the thick coat.

With a light touch of his middle finger, he wove his longish hair down onto his forehead, a strand or two mixing with his eyelashes.

As he fumbled for one of his mother's diamond earrings, he let his tongue explore his mouth, sensually, his fingers skirting over a bar of soap, over the soft bristles of a hair-brush, until they finally closed around one of the jewels. With the pear-shaped diamond in place, he moved back to the toilet where he sat stiffly, contemplating his image, first in one mirror, then another, the only movement the gentle swaying of the earring.

"Raphael, aren't you finished with your bath?"

"Almost." He quickly folded his young cock and balls underneath him, then he slowly parted his legs. Only a tuft of sandy pubic hair showed.

During the holidays, reservations were supposedly hard to come by at Tavern on the Green, but Kathryn wheedled her way into a table for two at ten PM. As for the lateness of the dinner hour, who cared? It was New York, wasn't it? And it was Central Park at Christmas.

So there they sat, against the window which looked out onto the parking lot and the skeletal trees whose iced branches, ablaze with tiny golden lights, shone against the drifting night clouds. But inside all was warm. Kathryn hadn't touched her food, but talked incessantly.

"Your daddy has had his hands in so many people's pockets for so long that he's turned into a bold son of a bitch and doesn't even bother to leave them with the lining anymore. They fall for that confident smile of his, they can't wait for him to fleece them. You'd think astute businessmen like Walter Newton and Theo Youngman would treat him like a leper after what he's done to them." She lifted the bottle of champagne from the bucket. Immediately a waiter was at her side to do the honors. "No, I can manage." She laughed. "You can't stand by my side all night." The waiter smiled in deference and moved away. She refilled her glass. "Maybe they figure if they let a Vice-President of Chase Manhattan Bank rob them, it gives them a kind of status. It couldn't happen to just anybody. Hoodwinked by the best of them."

Raphael made little pricks with his fork into the skin of the roast goose.

"Don't do that."

Raphael put his fork on his plate and stared at the white rose in the center of the table.

"Oh, yes," Kathryn continued, "David Hurst is the original Robber Baron and anybody from hell to breakfast is fair game to him."

Raphael gazed around the restaurant which was crowded

to the hilt.

"Quit looking around. Do you want to attract attention? What if we're being followed? Your daddy will stop at nothing." She frowned. "The divorce should be finalized soon, except for one little item: your daddy will try to get permanent custody of you. We might have to pretend to give in. I'll sign a paper. What's a paper, after all? Nothing that can't be ripped in two and thrown to the winds. That's the trouble with your daddy, he's lived his life thinking that a signature on a piece of paper is binding."

The scent from the roses lingered over Raphael's crystal water glass. Rose water. Raphael yawned.

"I should get quite a settlement so we can really live in luxury. Lots of lovely stocks and bonds. We'll never come back from Europe. Never. Do you understand, Raphael?"

"I do."

"And not a word to anyone about our plans."

"I won't say anything."

"Oh, God," Kathryn kept swallowing champagne. "I just couldn't have spent Christmas under his roof. I don't care how many tantrums he throws. It's much better, just the two of us, right here." She put her hands over her eyes and the pearl ring on her finger seemed to be a crystal ball she was consulting. "Sometimes your mother feels so alone, like she was on a train all by herself, wandering from car to car, with plenty of beautiful scenery to stare at, but not another human face anywhere, just empty seats. And all the time, the train is moving, moving, moving." The crystal ball cleared and her hands came down. "But it's all a silly nightmare. I open my eyes and there you are."

Raphael smiled.

"Now I guess I can eat something." Kathryn seemed relieved and exhausted at the same time. She took a small, tentative bite of Chicken Kiev.

Outside, heavy wet flakes had begun to fall, the kind Raphael knew would quickly accumulate. The snow had begun to dust the half dozen limos parked in the lot.

Raphael watched the drivers come grudgingly awake, nudge the caps back from their eyes, and step out into the cold to clear off the windshields. Only one of the men had been awake, smoking and reading a newspapaer, but now he too stepped outside, flicking his cigarette into the damp bushes and passing the newspaper to one of the others.

Once outside, the drivers seemed rejuvenated, leaning against the warmed-up engines, sharing jokes with each other, cursing the snow, anxious for their employers to leave the restaurant so they could get a leg up on the storm.

In a reverie, Raphael saw Peter in the lot resting against their limo, cap pulled down over his forehead, arms folded, waiting, quiet. Raphael's fingers touched one of the white roses in the vase before him. Peter slowly raised his head and tipped his cap to Raphael who approached, shivering, without a coat. There was a fleeting puzzlement that passed across Peter's face, then it was gone and he straightened like a stick, towering over the boy. He said nothing but opened the back door for Raphael to climb inside, his eyes all the while on the icy branches and the black sky; as he began to shut the door, Raphael touched his arm. Embarrassed, Peter glanced over his shoulder to see if anyone was watching. They were alone. From behind his back, Raphael pulled the white rose which he pressed into Peter's hand. Gruffly, Peter accepted it and as he closed his fist around it, the petals turned a bright red.

With a gesture of finality, Kathryn dropped her napkin by the side of her plate. "I'm dying to get back to the hotel and you'll soon see why. We can have our dessert later. We'll phone room service around midnight and have them bring us some hot chocolate and biscuits." She giggled. "We can even invite that funny man who plays the violin by the coatroom to come up and entertain us. We can do whatever we want!"

In the cab ride back to the hotel, Raphael watched the streetlights stripe his mother, who had fallen asleep, her head tilted back on the seat at a slightly awkward angle. The lights went down her dress in even lines and Raphael thought she resembled a gentle zebra. Her breathing was very soft like the snow that was blanketing Manhattan, and her profile was sharp as the ice that was building underneath the drift.

"Surprise, darling!" Kathryn switched on the light to reveal an eight-foot Christmas tree, fully decorated, surrounded by dozens of immaculately wrapped presents. Raphael, mildly astonished, approached the tree warily, breathing in the December scent of the pine needles. "While the two cats were away," Kathryn continued, tossing her mink over a lacquered Chinese chest, "the mice from downstairs were setting it up as directed."

"Mother, you shouldn't have gone to all the trouble."

"It wasn't any trouble, just expensive. But Christmas isn't the time to pinch pennies."

Raphael touched one of the ornaments, a half moon made of glass, delicately painted a powder blue.

Kathryn slipped her arm around her son's waist. "Your mommy wouldn't let Christmas go by without you having your very own tree."

"It's wonderful, really."

"I thought you'd be pleased." Kathryn moved to the bar where she poured herself a brandy. "Would you like anything, milk or a Coke?"

Raphael shook his head.

She slipped off her shoes. "I hope that sullen Jamaican maid — what was her name?"

"Annie."

"I hope Annie will sweep up the pine needles that drop off in the night. The heat in here will make them brittle. I'll have to leave a note to remind her." She gave Raphael a pinch on the cheek. "The presents are mostly all from me, but I managed to pack one or two small things from your aunts and uncles before Peter drove us to the station."

"I haven't bought you a present yet."

"I don't want you going out on your own. Anyway, I don't need one. This is my present. You and me alone. Free." She sank onto the sofa and put her legs up on the coffee table. "Will you bring me my pills?"

Her pillbox was next to the red ice lipstick which was still open, a mountain peak on the flat bathroom vanity.

"And a glass of water," Kathryn called. "The brandy's

finished."

Raphael filled the glass to the brim, trying to see his reflection in it. He thought he saw his eye floating but when he blinked the water was clear.

Kathryn swallowed five of her snowpills, as Raphael called them, then asked him to light some candles. The room became soft and magical. Raphael sat cross-legged in front of the tree, and his mother's voice emerged soft and lulling behind him as if she were telling a Christmas story, but it was only one of her usual complaints about his father.

The gaily wrapped boxes were vying for his attention; they spilled down on top of each other like building blocks carelessly toppled by a child. For some reason, Raphael was attracted to a thin, bright green package whose card, upside down, was dimly lit by the snowy light outside. Raphael deciphered the topsy-turvy signature to read, "To Raphael, From Peter." Though his heart leapt, he knew he had to be mistaken. He gingerly extricated the package and turned it around right. The card read, "To Raphael, From Uncle Bertram." No doubt a tie, a Scottish plaid, of the ilk Bertram gave his nephews every Christmas.

If only Peter had a gift for him somewhere under the tree. A pair of black silk panties. A bottle of heady perfume. "To Raphael, From Peter."

Kathryn's voice was now a wind sound, a whisper addressed to no one at all. As soon as she was asleep, Raphael crawled onto the bed in the alcove and began counting sheep, well-fed, placid sheep, bounding over a wooden gate onto a twilit snowy embankment.

Even from across the room, Raphael knew something was wrong. His mother's arm hung stiffly and unnaturally off the side of the sofa, her fingers dangling onto the carpet. Her legs were spread apart and her hair had become undone, cascading over her face. He approached her prudently, as if he were stealing up on one of his presents on Christmas morning. He was relieved to hear her breathing, although it was very labored. When he shook her gently, there was no reply. Her face was red and inflated, like a powder puff. He phoned the downstairs desk.

After the house doctor had examined her and called for an ambulance, he turned to Raphael. "Your mother needs to go to the hospital right away." The doctor took a tissue and wiped the bottom of his shoe. He had inadvertently crushed the pillbox which had been lying on the floor next to the sofa, and had ground the colored dust of the pills into the carpet. "Looks to me as if she's had a bad reaction to drugs or alcohol. Or both." He picked up the empty brandy glass and handed it to Raphael. "I've no way of knowing right now how serious this is, if there are any complications . . ." Raphael put the glass on top of the bar. "We might have to pump her stomach." Raphael kept his back turned. "Will you come along in the ambulance?"

"No, I'd better stay here."

"Yes, you're right. No need you sitting there in the corridor getting all nervous. Stay here and rest. We'll phone you as soon as we can make a diagnosis. Now about that number . . ."

Raphael had promised the doctor Uncle Bertram's phone

number, which he wrote on a slip of hotel note paper.

Before the attendants lifted Kathryn onto the stretcher, Raphael knelt and kissed her hand. Then they were gone.

Raphael opened the curtains and sun filled up the room. He stood there, aching in the brightness, confused as to what he should do next. The traffic noises below broke any coherent thought in two, so he just gave up.

He ran himself a hot bath and relaxed in the tub, lying there until the water was colder than he was, then he toweled himself dry and combed his hair back. Finding his skin a bit pallid, he gave his cheeks a touch of rouge. He drifted into the suite. He pulled out a 3 by 5 index card from his wallet. It was folded in half. He uncreased it and laid it on the bureau. On it was the ornate handwriting, already fading, of an associate of his father's:

Particulars:
Name: PETER JAMES RYMER
Age: 28
Birthplace: Syracuse, New York
Height: 6'1"
Weight: Approx. 180 lbs.
Hair: Dark brown. Mustache too.
Eyes: Hazel
Employed by me for past four years
Excellent chauffeur
Polite. Honest. Discreet. Friendly. Well-liked by family.
No traffic violations
No history of arrests — felony or misdemeanor
Recommended without reservation

The lake was frozen over and the tuft of earth that served
as a small island in the middle was an icy brown, an even mix-
ture of rocks and earth. Peter skipped a stone onto the lake.
In summer he would have had the pleasure of seeing it disappear in several diminishing splashes; now his enjoyment
was auditory, hearing the ricocheting stone make several
gunshot bursts and then skid along and stop at the edge of
the ice.

Duke, the Scottish terrier, poked his nose with some interest at the frozen reeds and the rifts in the frigid earth and
never failed to be startled at the stones as they hit the ice.
After awhile he looked imploringly at Peter, his breath hanging in the still air, his ears cocked in anticipation of Peter's
whistling, signaling that it was time to return to the house.
But Peter was watching a figure approaching at a brisk clip
down the long drive. It was Gina Brown, the Hursts' maid,
having just gotten off the bus from Tarrytown.

"Any word on them?" Gina asked, breathless as she caught
up to Peter and put her hand on his jacket.

"None as far as Mr. Hurst said anything to me."

Gina was young, her face still prey to outbreaks of acne,
her voice still that of a green schoolgirl. She brushed her
thick blond hair away from her face and stood with her
mouth open, her eyes traveling helplessly from Peter to
Duke and back again. She had witnessed some unusual and
uncomfortable scenes among the Hurst family in her two
years working for them, especially between husband and
wife, but this was the first time two members, mother and

son, had up and left the three-member family, just up and left, as she had told her husband the previous night, without a word.

"Come on, Duke," Peter finally spoke. The dog was chewing on some red berries, the only color in the drab landscape. Gina went over to the terrier and gave his collar a tug. But Duke, so eager to leave moments ago, had changed his mind, such was his fascination with the berries. "Don't force him, Gina. Let's just walk up to the house. He'll follow."

The Hursts' Westchester mansion loomed in front of them, the sun's sinking light giving the tall, spotless windows a rosy luster. The twenty-eight rooms that made up the three floors, basement and attic, was a ludicrous amount of space for David, Kathryn and Raphael, and for Peter and the cook, Vi Hanson. The other two staff members employed by the Hursts, Gina, and Walt Riponte, the gardener and handyman, lived in their own houses.

To Peter, the mansion was a pretty depressing place in the winter, but he never voiced his opinion to Vi or Gina or anyone else. After all, he had taken this position, and the winter blues came with the territory.

There was a knocking on the inside of the study window. Through the sunny sheen, Peter saw David Hurst motioning him to come inside. Peter nodded then looked around. Sure enough, Duke was bounding towards them, and Gina's voice floated over the stillness, "Good dog! Good, good dog!" Peter and Gina let the terrier in through the kitchen door, then Peter stepped a few doors down into the study.

David Hurst stood with his back to Peter. He stared out,

evidently at his expanse of frozen property, and was reluctant to tear his eyes away even though he knew the man he had summoned was waiting for him.

"Cold out still?" Hurst finally asked without turning around.

"Same as the last few days. Chilly, sir."

"Hmm. Well, where the hell has my wife taken herself and my son to now?" He turned around and his eyes, instead of appearing dreamy and satisfied from studying nature, were impatient and angry, filled with an internal brooding. "What time did you take them to the train station?"

"Yesterday morning, sir, around nine o'clock. They boarded the 9:25 for New York City."

"I see. We've been over this before, I know, Peter, but they didn't tell you where they were going to be staying?"

"No, sir."

"And you didn't happen to overhear anything that might have suggested their hotel or other lodgings?"

"I didn't hear their conversation."

"I'll be damned." They could hear the dog barking in the kitchen and Gina's attempts to quiet him. "Listen, Peter, I want you and Gina to search my wife's room and my son's room. See if you can find any notes left behind that might have an address or phone number. And see if you can discover if they took anything out of the ordinary that might suggest a more permanent departure than I'm imagining. For instance, did my wife take every bag she owned . . . that kind of thing. Gina would be apt to know."

"Yes, sir."

David laughed ironically as he watched Peter leave the room. Perhaps the trouble had begun the day he had announced Peter's imminent arrival to his wife.

It had been in the spring and he had been standing in this very study. He had been reading the 3 by 5 index card listing Peter Rymer's qualifications, and Kathryn had come in, taken the card from his hands, and given it a breezy once-over.

She had addressed him with a mocking innocence. "But he sounds too perfect, darling. Too perfect for words."

She had hesitated for a bit of drama, then crossed the room and, taking little puffs of breath, had inched the monumental Ming vase, which sat on the floor and whose lip brushed her waist, out of the direct sunlight. Her task completed, she had raised her hands imploringly and purred, "Everybody has something wrong with them!"

"They certainly do," David had replied as he left the room. "It's all a matter of degree, isn't it?"

The next day David Soule Hurst had filed for divorce from his wife of eighteen years, Kathryn Masares Hurst, at the offices of his attorney on Madison Avenue and 32nd Street.

David heard Peter and Gina mount the stairs, heading toward Kathryn's and Raphael's rooms. He turned back to his picture window and looked outside at nothing in particular.

"She's taken some of her nicest clothes and jewelry, but not all by any means," Gina whispered, ill at ease at her task.

Peter had been through every drawer in Kathryn's desk and gone through her address book, which she hadn't taken, but he hadn't found a clue as to their whereabouts.

Scattered about the room were snapshots, most of them of Raphael: Raphael playing in his bubble bath, at the stables with his cousins, drinking iced tea on the terrace out back, Vi proudly presenting him with a piece of chocolate cake. But in all the photographs Raphael had a distant gaze. Peter thought Raphael must have been taken by surprise when the pictures had been developed and he had found himself the subject. As far as Peter was concerned, Raphael looked as if he hadn't been there at all.

Raphael was a strange bird, no two ways about it, thought Peter, and he felt that same sentiment moments later even more strongly when, on entering Raphael's room, he saw something black protruding from under the pillows of his unmade bed. Without forming an image in his mind, he knew deep down what it was. Still, he was astonished when he pulled the pillow up and found his pair of leather driving gloves that he thought he had misplaced last summer.

Peter was too stunned to make an inventory of the room. He let Gina do it. Then he and Gina reported to Mr. Hurst that they had found no number, no address, and that only two bags each and a minimum of clothes and personal items were missing. Then he made his way to his room in the attic.

He turned on the lamp, as it was dark now, and laid the gloves gently in his drawer. Peter Rymer was a meticulous man. He decided to polish his several pairs of shoes. He spent an hour spiffing them up so that, when he held them under the lamp, he couldn't see a mark on them. He put the business of finding his gloves under Raphael's pillow out of his mind; but first he dismissed any culpability on Raphael's part — after all, Raphael might have found them anywhere in the house and not known they were Peter's. Peter had never said anything to anyone about them being missing. Raphael had simply kept them for himself. He had probably laid them out on the bed as a possibility to take with him yesterday but had discarded them at the last minute and hadn't had time to return them to his drawer.

Diregarding the fact that it was winter, Peter liked his job with the Hursts immensely. He was treated with respect and had the whole attic — one long room with a TV which he watched occasionally and a CD player which he never listened to — to himself. Vi prepared all his meals and was an excellent cook. And his wages were more than fair.

He read newpapers and magazines and kept a stack near the sofa. He kept his personal papers, his stamp collection, and his clothes in a wall unit. In one corner was a carousel horse that no one wanted or knew where it had come from. Probably from previous owners. But Peter liked the white horse with the golden saddle and bridle and sometimes before bed crossed the room to give it a gentle squeeze on the ears.

It was a dark night; the moon hadn't yet put in an appearance. Peter turned on all three lights in his room but they didn't dispel the somberness of the winter's night. He was getting hungry so he was glad when Vi buzzed him for dinner. Gina said good-night and walked off to the bus stop while Peter and Vi ate quietly in the kitchen. David Hurst dined alone in his study.

Raphael opened the closet door and located a simple beige dress that his mother complained had been too bulky for her. He struggled into it. It pinched him and only came down to the knees, but he was able to zip it all the way up the back. Then he put on some hose and his penny loafers. He fixed an onyx brooch to his breast and shook his hair down over his eyes.

"I didn't know anyone was inside," he heard the island drawl apologize. "You should have the Do Not Disturb sign up."

Raphael didn't reply.

"Shall I go ahead and clean up?"

He nodded and moved to the window, staring across at the building opposite, its roof punctuated by strange little gargoyles. Annie, meanwhile, began dusting the furniture with peacock feathers. "Crimeny, you already made the bed," he heard her mutter sourly.

"It saves you the work." He kept his eyes on the frozen gargoyles.

"Saves me the work?" she ridiculed him. "I brought you up new sheets. Now I have to unmake the bed and strip it down, then put the clean ones on."

"Don't bother. The sheets weren't slept on last night."

He could feel her eyes on him. She continued to dust quietly. He heard her pick up the brandy glass on the bar, then head into the bathroom. He sat daintily on the sofa, nervously drumming his fingers on the cushion. When Annie came out of the bathroom, she stopped dead in her tracks and burst out laughing, "You're the boy, aren't you, who's staying here with his mama?"

"That's right."

"Mary, mother of Jesus, you make a pretty girl. You look about fourteen, with little melon breasts. Where's your mama?"

"I don't want to talk about her. She's sick. It makes me very sad."

After a beat, Annie shrewdly dumped her maid's cargo by the door, then sat down next to Raphael. "How long you been passin', honey?"

"I don't know what you mean."

"Back in Kingston, we had a lot of boys who could pass. That is," she cackled, "up until the last minute. Then there was trouble. Big trouble . . . A lot of them couldn't pass, though. They did too much, too much lipsticks, crazy colored wigs. Like birds flying into a hurricane. But you," she ran her fingers through Raphael's hair, "are perfect. You don't have no extra baggage. You look like a sweet little girl."

Raphael moved away.

"Don't you take offence," Annie scolded, clasping the hem of Raphael's beige dress between her two fingers. "You don't have to feel funny in front of me. I don't care one way or another. What's your name again, honey?"

He hesitated, then, "Raphael."

"Raphael. That's right. I remember your mama saying that name over and over. She sure didn't seem to have no use for me. 'Annie, do this, that and the other.' Oh — sorry to bring Miss Mama up." Her tone became golden. "You say, honey, your mama took sick? And left you here all alone?"

Raphael nodded.

"Well, you cheer up. Let the sunshine in your heart."

Raphael frowned.

"No use being lonely during the holidays. Tell you what, you and me will go downstairs and have us a nice fancy lunch. You miss your mama? Well, I miss mine too though she's been in her grave ten years." She jumped up excitedly and whipped into the bathroom. "You don't mind if I make my lips red and use some perfume?"

Raphael shrugged, crossing his legs.

"Come on, boy, and help me find something to put on."

They selected an orange taffeta dress and a dark red wig. Annie shrieked with delight as she threw a fox stole around her shoulders and squared a fox-trimmed hat with a smart black veil on her head. Kathryn's jewelry box lay open on the bureau and Annie chose a bracelet of gold leaves and clasped it on her wrist.

She insisted they walk down the stairs instead of using the elevator, in case she should be recognized by other maids on the floors. She led the way down, flight after flight, thumping the bannister for emphasis as she talked. "We make a wicked pair, you so white and me so black. There haven't been two ladies dressed so much like sunshine this side of my old church in Kingston. We'd sure set those pews on fire, make that stained glass go pale."

They were seated at the edge of the court where egotistical poinsettias shielded them from the lobby.

Mistletoe hung from the chandeliers. "Don't you get any

ideas, boy," Annie crowed. "You stay the way you are, like a soft, colored confection."

When the waiter appeared, he didn't look twice at Raphael whose transformation was miraculously subtle, but he did raise his eyebrows at Annie.

"We would like, sir, two roast beef dinners with shrimp to start and plenty of champagne," she said.

"Would Madam care to make a selection from our wine list?"

"No, just bring us the two most expensive bottles of champagne in this hotel and make sure they're chilly as an iceberg."

"Madam is staying with us?"

"No, she is." Annie jerked her thumb at Raphael.

"I see." The waiter vacillated but was worn down by Raphael's glacial stare. He put in their order.

"I'll do the talking," Annie was quick to size up the situation. "You be the little princess."

Annie devoured both portions of shrimp, castigating Raphael for not eating his fair share. "You don't know what you're missing, boy. These still have the sea in their souls."

"Why would you think that, Annie?"

"Why not? There's a soul in everything, in the sea, in the sky, in a rock baked by the sun, in the specks of dust I have to sweep up all the time." She giggled. "Some rooms sure have more dust souls than others, my peacock feathers know which ones they are. And see, even those feathers got souls."

Raphael finished half his roast beef dinner before delegating it to Annie.

"You're making me crazy, picking at your food like that. Don't you want to feed those two breasts of yours, get them nice and plump?" When Raphael blushed, she had a good laugh. "You're a shy little sweetmeat. You been raised just right. Now, drink your champagne."

"I've never been allowed to have any."

"You're a princess. You must learn to drink champagne." She poured Raphael a glass. "Sip it slowly, like a lady. There are two souls in champagne, one in the bubbles themselves and one that always stays behind in the glass, reminding you that it should never stay empty or the soul's gonna wither and die."

Raphael took one sip, then another. His throat burned but he liked the taste.

Winking, Annie patted his hand. "I'd love to bundle you up and take you back to Kingston with me. I'd dress you up, comb your heavenly hair, take you with me into the church. Those other gals would hold on tight to their men when they saw you coming," she chuckled.

For dessert there was baked Alaska.

"It's really too sweet," Annie decided. "I like something with more bite."

They were dazed by the champagne. Raphael saw thousands of poinsettia leaves circling in his head. His stomach felt queasy.

"Ah, Raphael, what a wonderful lunch." Annie drew the fox fur tight around her shoulders. When the waiter presented them with the bill, she nudged Raphael under the table. "Show him your room key, honey."

Raphael produced the key and had to sign a wobbly name under a five-hundred-dollar figure.

"Very good, miss," the waiter smiled. "Merry Christmas."

"Merry Christmas," Raphael and Annie said in unison.

Annie itched the skin under the gold bracelet. "I have to go powder my face. Then we'll go back upstairs." As she swept off, she kissed Raphael on the cheek, leaving a lipstick mark in the rouge.

He sat for an eternity, waiting, the waving poinsettia leaves resembling Annie's feather duster.

Finally, the waiter appeared before him and cleared his throat. "Are you waiting for your friend?"

"Yes."

"I don't know if you should still expect her, miss. She went out through the hotel entrance onto the street some time ago."

Raphael funneled his gaze through the poinsettias to the lobby's swinging gold doors. "In the snow?"

"Yes, she went out into the snow, miss."

"Oh . . ."

The elevator seemed to take off like a spaceship. Raphael steadied himself against the mirror so that he wouldn't faint.

"Seven." The elevator man pulled back the glass.

"Thank you," Raphael said in slow motion while several impatient guests stood aside as he wafted off.

He threw himself on the bed, which he had discovered after a long search, and stared up at the ceiling. He wished that he and Peter were standing, hand in hand, in the shadows of Westminster Abbey. His hand ran along his dress until it closed over the onyx brooch; he was holding onto something, at least, and with that security, he allowed himself to pass out.

It wasn't until close to midnight that he regained consciousness, and at last everything had stopped spinning. As he crossed to the bathroom, he noticed half a dozen messages pushed under the door. Dated at hour intervals they all said the same thing: *Raphael. Urgent! Your mother all right. Please call her at the hospital.* Not at this hour. Tomorrow would be soon enough. He pulled off her dress and, relieved that she was better, tenderly smoothed the material and hung it back in the closet. The hose came off next, then his loafers. He washed his face free of the traces of rouge and of Annie's lipstick, then wandered naked to the window. The snow had stopped but the gargoyles were still dusted with it and thick icicles hung from their wings and noses. Raphael threw himself face down on the sofa.

It had been a summer's afternoon, the shadows of everything and everyone lengthening and the smell of the wild raspberries and the green grass giving a sense of pleasure and well-being. They were playing croquet; Raphael and his cousins, Hannah and Mary, against the older contingent, Uncle Bertram, his wife, Nan, and Raphael's father. Kathryn sat under an elm tree, pulling grass and thinking that the shadows of the trees looked like people sneaking slowly up on the croquet players.

Inside the kitchen, Vi commented to Peter, who had just come inside from polishing the limo, "That's the silliest game

I ever saw. Clumsy. Putting those big balls through the wickets with rainbow-colored sledgehammers."

"It's a fun game," Peter said, wiping his brow with a dish towel and stepping outside. "It's just that they don't seem to have gotten the hang of it."

Kathryn waved to Peter from across the lawn and Peter waved back, kneeling down in a clover patch to watch the progress of the game.

Raphael had been lucky enough to knock his opponents out of the way and now had a clear, though long, shot through the center wicket. He stood there, confused. From the corner of his eye he saw Peter watching. Peter gave him the thumbs-up sign. Raphael shut his eyes and in the blackness Peter approached and asked him, "May I?" When Raphael assented, to everyone's surprise but his, Peter enfolded him in his arms and showed him how to aim for the wicket. Together they took a firm but easy swing and the ball went through. Raphael opened his eyes and took a swing. The ball went far wide of the wicket, yet Raphael could still feel Peter's strong arms around his chest.

The oldsters won and the youngsters, Mary and Hannah being several years younger than Raphael, went down together to the brook where a rope swing with a carved oak seat hung over the shallow water.

"Come on, Raphael, we'll push you first."

And in the still twilight, the girls pushed their cousin higher and higher.

It had been summer and the smell of things that belonged to the twilight had given him a sense of pleasure and well-

being.

Raphael's fingers traced patterns on the carpet. There was still evidence of his mother's snowpills that the doctor had ground into the weave. Raphael sat up and stretched, then poured himself a brandy from the bar. He just sipped at it.

Not too much later, he descended to the lobby in the elevator, the mirror sending him back a different image than the one this afternoon. This time it was a handsome young man in blue jeans and a black cashmere sweater, a grey silk scarf around his neck, yet under the clothes he was the same Raphael.

He heard a woman's deep-toned voice negotiating a syncopated version of *Silent Night*. He wandered into the intimate club off the side of the dining room where he could see the embodiment of the voice, a heavy woman in a royal blue, sequined gown, multicolored rings on every finger.

The bartender was surprised when Raphael settled on one of the stools. "Thirty dollar cover charge tonight and the show's almost over . . . And you're underage."

Raphael presented his room key.

The bartender shrugged. "What'll you have?"

"Nothing."

"What are you, a wise guy?" he hissed. He checked his watch. "It's Christmas Eve, that's when they all start crawling out of the woodwork."

The woman had slowed the carol, turning it blue. The flecks of dust stirring in the spotlight looked like snow that had materialized at her command. "All is calm . . ." The flakes settled softly on her blonde wig. "All . . . all is bright . . ." Though she moved from table to table, her mind didn't seem to be on her audience, her eyes were distant, visionary, her fingers traveling with the fluidity of the notes on the backup piano. She was nearly touching Raphael. "It was a silent . . . an, oh, so silent night . . ."

After the crowd had left and the waiters were clearing off the tables, Raphael made his way to the corner booth where the singer was spraying her throat with a foul-smelling mist. Raphael rocked from one foot to the other, his hands behind his back.

Puzzled, she droppped the mist into her bag. "Do I know you?"

He shook his head.

"Well, would you like to sit down?"

Loosening his scarf, he slid in beside her.

"You were watching the show from the bar."

He nodded.

"I hate to see anyone drinking alone on Christmas Eve."

"I wasn't really drinking."

"We'll fix that. Hey, Ed, bring my pal a cognac. Same as mine." The bartender nodded, blowing a smoke ring her way.

"What's your name?" she asked.

"Raphael."

"Raphael, I'm glad you came over. I had nothing to do except polish my rings. My valueless glass rings. My name's Leah Martin. Ever heard of me?"

"No."

"That's all right. No one else has either. Except a couple of

crummy managers who manage to squeeze me in someplace
when a signed headliner gets sick." The room lights dimmed,
leaving only the spots on the small stage at full power.
"Thank God," she cried. "I wanted to be a star all my life, but
I sure hate bright lights."

Ed put Raphael's cognac in front of him.

"What do you think, Ed, I'm really robbing the cradle
tonight, huh?"

"Not really, Leah. I saw a ten-year-old get on the elevator
with his mother. I could try and get his room number."

Leah laughed, a deep, happy sound. "Let's try him next
year."

"Why give him a chance to grow up?" Ed replied, moving
away.

"That guy gives me bad dreams," Leah said.

Raphael dipped his tongue into the cognac.

"Are you staying at this hotel?"

"Yes."

"By yourself?"

He paused. "Yes."

"What, young man, are you doing down here at this time
of night?"

"My room was lonely."

"All rooms are lonely. This one is too, even when it's full of
people, even when I'm singing to them. Lonely is skin.
Lonely is a state of mind."

Raphael studied her, more carefully. The royal blue gown
grasped her so tightly that it seemed to be punishing her. She
had the kind of plump face that thwarted age and rerouted

lines of anxiety to someplace well hidden.

"Now that we've cleared that up, why do you have lonely skin, Raphael?"

He thought of himself being pulled from his mother's womb with lonely skin for the world to see. The doctor slapped his bottom, but kept his eyes discreetly turned away. Kathryn clothed him immediately as he cried on her breast, so his father, Aunt Nan and Uncle Bertram wouldn't know. The nurses, cooing over him, gazed at the ceiling. "I guess I was born that way."

Leah sighed. "This doesn't sound good. You're too young to talk like that. You have a whole life ahead to screw up. You got to start with a cleaner slate." She dipped a handkerchief into her cognac and began to polish a red glass ring.

"See, you won't look at my lonely skin either," he said.

Leah whipped her head up and glared at Raphael. "I'll look at your lonely skin, anytime, baby. You have beautiful, sweet skin, I can smell it from here. You don't know what the fuck you're talking about, you beautiful son of a bitch. I know what lonely skin looks like. I've seen it around . . . You ain't got it . . ."

Raphael burst into a smile, in spite of himself.

"Now, do you mind if I finish polishing my ring?"

"Go ahead." He took another sip.

Leah hummed snippets of blues, Broadway tunes, lullabyes. Then she stopped suddenly. "Ever been in love, Raphael?"

"No."

"That's usually at the bottom of everything." She began

sliding the rings back on her fingers.

Finally, Peter said with real confusion, "You're about as pretty as my girlfriend, you know that?" Raphael had felt faint and his throat too strangled to give a response.

"Well," he hedged. "Maybe I am in love . . ."

It had been a blustery night, the wind a mournful whip, Raphael its victim. His feet, sticking out from under the quilt, were cold even though it was late August. Kicking off the quilt, he crossed to the glass and drew back the curtains. Trees were bent in the wind, fighting to stay rooted. Clouds came in gusts on the wind, clouds that changed shape in the moonlight and seemed to graze the top of the mansion with their misty veils. Leaves blew and caught in the corners of the windowpanes, and somewhere there came the savage whistle of a train. Everything outside was alive in the dark. Raphael could even see the lake ripple when the moon was left to glitter between the gaps in the clouds.

Throwing on his robe, the purple Chinese silk robe with the peacocks etched in gold and silver, he ran down the hall, his bare feet warming as they grazed the floorboards.

The stairs to the attic were at the end of the hall and he put his hand on the bannister and paused. The hall at the top of the stairs outside Peter's room was dark. There was no light from under his door. Slowly Raphael made his way up the stairs. He paused on the small landing. The moon lit the round stained glass window, a painting of twelve turtledoves on a wide, fat tree against a gossamer background of azure blue. Though he couldn't see out, Raphael heard the wind rattle the panes and for a moment the doves seemed to stir and the branches creak.

On up the rest of the stairs to the narrow hallway. There on a low table was Peter's telephone and next to it Peter's black leather gloves and chauffeur's cap. Raphael picked up the gloves and gently rubbed them against his cheek. It was in these gloves that the whole night breathed.

Raphael stood outside Peter's door, breathless and silent. There was a sound from inside and then it was gone. Mattress springs? Footsteps? A window closing? Raphael pressed against the door, his heart beating on the wood.

From behind the door came a cry. A sob. Raphael sank to his knees, his robe unfolding like a Chinese fan. He put his eye to the keyhole. A wavering flame from a candle etched deep shadows on the wall. His eye found Peter's bed. There were two people in it, Peter and a woman, and they both were naked. Peter had penetrated the woman, whose face Raphael couldn't see, but he saw Peter lying between her legs, pumping into her, his ass thrashing up and down. There were moans, the sounds of lovemaking.

An hour passed with the quickness of a speeding dart and still Raphael was at the keyhole. Even when the candle had burned out there were still sobs and small astonished screams.

Raphael took his eye from the blackness and walked slowly down to the kitchen. He heated some hot chocolate and drank it quietly, listening to the dying wind and gazing with bitterness at the white china plates that hung in a row on nails.

A short time after the dawn had risen, Peter and the young

woman shuffled into the kitchen.

"You're up early," Peter greeted Raphael in surprise.

"Good morning," Raphael mumbled.

"I'll bring the car around," Peter said to the woman. "We'll get you home in no time."

The door slammed shut. The woman approached Raphael. She wore a plaid jumper and had long sandy hair and pink cheeks. "Hi," she said cheerfully. "I'm Susan, a friend of Peter's. You must be Raphael, I've heard a lot about you."

Raphael raised his head. Tears flowed down his face. "Why did you come here?"

"What? What did you say?"

The tears kept pouring down, spilling onto the table. "Why did you come here? . . . Why can't you leave us alone? . . ."

Leah tugged playfully at Raphael's scarf. "So you are in love," she said. "Who's the lucky girl?"

"Susan," Raphael muttered. He finished the last drop of cognac. His fingers made circles around the rim of the glass.

"You look pretty beat," Leah observed.

"I guess I am. I think I'll go up to my room and lie down. I wish you'd come up for a while."

Leah hesitated. Then, "Well, I do have some time to kill."

They stepped over the new batch of messages that had been slipped under the door.

"Ignore them," Raphael said.

Leah whistled. "I always wanted to see one of these

rooms. I could move in here for about a ten year stretch."

"Why don't you pour us something to drink?" Raphael rubbed his eyes. "There's the bar."

"I'm tanked up already."

"Me, too."

Raphael took a pair of red pyjamas from a drawer and walked into the bathroom where, half in slumber, he changed into them. Leah stood stiffly by the Christmas tree, watching him through the open door, flushed with desire for him. Her fingers absentmindedly pricked the ends of the pine needles. When he appeared before her, ready for bed, she bit her lip.

"Are you sure you wanted me to come up?" she asked slowly.

"Yes. I wanted to be tucked in."

Leah frowned, her fingers pulling on her sequins. "Tucked in?"

"Yes, I thought maybe you could tuck me in, then sit on the sofa till I fell asleep."

Leah's hands went to her hips. "Son of a bitch."

"You don't have to."

"Quit stating the obvious," she sighed. "I said I had some time to kill."

Raphael jumped into bed and Leah fluffed his pillows and covered him with the blanket.

"Leah?"

"What?"

"You're thinking the person I'm in love with is Susan, but it isn't, it's Peter."

Leah tugged harder on her sequins. "What's in a name?"

She turned out the light. "Now you get some sleep. You're whacked."

Raphael watched her for a long time, sitting there in the shadows, on the sofa, her hands folded quietly in her lap.

He drifted off.

Leah started to sweat, though she kept very still. She adjusted her blonde wig, pulling the corners down just above her ears. She thought with a kind of horrified amusement how her dark, curly hair lay in a tangle of bobby pins underneath and how when she got back to her house in West Orange her dog would bark at her warily as she sat in front of the mirror and undid the pins. Did she have enough milk in the house for herself? Enough bread and cheese? Did she have dog food for Rusty? The stores would be closed tomorrow. Every time Leah looked over at the sleeping boy, she felt a knot in her stomach.

Raphael had been asleep for some time when he heard the click of the door. "Now you go back to sleep, Raphael. I have to leave now." The insistent streams of dawn invaded the room.

"Leah?"

"Yeah."

"Don't go yet."

"I have to," the voice was tired. "I have to catch a bus."

"Stay."

"In a way, it's gonna be kind of hard, those few steps from here to the elevator. I'd like to stay and get to know you better, Raphael. But the Gods have other plans." She closed the door softly behind her.

"Daddy, this is Raphael."

"My God, where have you been?"

"I want to come home for Christmas."

"And your mother?"

"She's at New York Hospital recovering from a Christmas binge. But she's doing OK."

"She had too much to drink. Is that what you're saying?"

"Yes. Bertram must be with her, though I'm sure she's made him swear not to tell you."

"I see. And where are you?"

"In New York. At the Plaza. Can you send Peter for me? I'm just a couple of hours away."

"Of course, Raphael."

"I'll be down in the lobby at two, waiting."

Raphael took a hot bath. The tenseness that had been building in him ebbed, then disappeared with the water down the drain. He gave his clean, shiny hair a few dozen strokes with the brush, then dabbed some perfume behind his ears and smoothed his cheeks with rouge. He put on his dark blue suit, slipped his mother's pear-shaped diamond earrings into his pocket, packed his bag, phoned Alitalia, then went down to the lobby to wait for Peter.

Peter Rymer entered, moving through the hotel's revolving doors like no other man on earth, with an aura of assurance and relaxed masculinity that Raphael had only seen in certain men in Hollywood movies of the thirties.

"Raphael," Peter knelt in front of the big easy chair in which Raphael was sitting, "you gave your father a pretty bad time."

"It wasn't my fault."

"I know. He doesn't blame you. Come on, then. Let's go. The sooner we get on the road, the sooner the two of you can start your Christmas together. Are these your only bags?"

"Yes."

Peter whisked them up and led Raphael out of the hotel. Then he settled the boy in the back of the limo and started to drive north on Madison Avenue. Raphael swallowed hard and pretended to look at the shop windows.

Peter glanced back in the rearview mirror at Raphael whose face was flushed. He returned Peter's stare with passive intensity.

"Find a spot to pull over, Peter," Raphael commanded.

Peter frowned. "Are you crazy? There's nowhere to park around here. What's the matter?"

"Look. Turn down a side street or find a garage, but do something. I have to talk to you."

Peter found an alleyway which he blocked. "We can't stay here very long."

"We won't have to." Raphael's face brightened. "We're going to Rome this afternoon. We'll leave the limo at Kennedy Airport. There's an Alitalia flight at six o'clock."

"What are you talking about?"

Raphael waved his mother's pear-shaped diamonds in Peter's face. "We'll put the tickets on the family credit card and when we get to Rome we'll sell these. They're worth thousands of dollars."

Peter brushed the diamonds away from his face. "Put

those back in your bag."

But Raphael wasn't listening. "We'll rent a villa on the Mediterranean. Just us. No one else around."

"Raphael." Peter's voice was low and angry.

"You know the kind of place, with beautiful flowers spilling down the walls. We'll swim in the sea all day long if we want to and let the sun take its time drying us off. Or we could go on picnics in the mountains, or visit the vineyards. Or medieval towns. Would you like that?"

"Raphael . . ." The voice had lost none of its heat.

"Let me finish. At night we'll stand on our terrace and watch the moon come up out of the water. And we'll watch its reflection, all silvery and ghostly, as it climbs into the sky. We'll go to bed then. And we'll hold each other all night long. And when the sun comes up, we'll know . . . we'll know another day is waiting for us just like the one before."

Peter, anxiously stroking his moustache, pulled his cap low on his forehead and started the car. "We're going home now, Raphael. Your father is waiting for you."

But Raphael threw his arm around Peter's neck. "I want to be your girl. I'll be good to you."

Peter knocked his arm away. "No. You're going home now."

Raphael escaped from the car before Peter had a chance to lock the doors. He heard Peter desperately calling after him but he ran like a rocket until there was no voice calling him anymore. He turned onto Fifth Avenue, then he slowed down. Panting, he found himself sidestepping a few tourists fascinated by some elegant display windows. He steadied himself against one of the windows and brushed his hair off the lapel of his dark blue suit.

Kicking aside the slew of new urgent messages, he found his way to the bathroom where he splashed cold water on his face, which seemed to scare away an oncoming headache. He put on a coat of pink lipstick and a bit more perfume behind his ears. Then he poured himself a brandy. Snow was melting all over the city, and on the roof of the building opposite water was running off the backs of the gargoyles. His feet were wet so he slipped off his shoes and rubbed his toes together.

Kathryn was probably due to return soon, David would be phoning, Peter would be pounding at the door.

Raphael dropped on the sofa. He sipped his brandy. His pink lips had left ghosts on the glass. If they could only leave their ghosts on Peter's skin . . . They were standing together on their terrace, the dazzling blue of the Mediterranean everywhere they looked . . . Peter's arms were folded around his chest . . . Raphael refused to cut it out of his heart, he had to at least keep a beggar's hope that one day, it might really happen.

All the unopened presents lay glittering beneath the tree, at the top of which reigned a gossamer-haired angel Raphael had never particularly noticed before. The cherub was robed in white linen, and his round, placid face, his blue crystal eyes, spoke of paradise.

The boy leaned back against the sofa and, looking into the angel's face, said one word, "Raphael . . ."

LIGHTS OF BROADWAY

VAL HATTAUER PAUSED IN THE ENTRYWAY OF THE PALACE Theater, staring at three sets of double doors that led into the lobby. Finally he approached the middle ones and gave them a gentle push. Nothing.

"All locked up, Bud," the janitor sweeping up the corners informed him.

"When do they open them?"

"Oh, not till much later. Closer to showtime. If you want to see somebody in the show, try going around to the back door."

"I don't want to see anybody."

Shrugging, the janitor turned back to the corners.

Val glanced around him. A middle-aged woman with jet black hair sat inside the ticket booth, spitting out information to the line of customers without ever so much as glancing up from the task of filing her nails. A pro, Val thought.

He stepped outside onto Broadway, where the autumn wind made him curse, and set down his paper bag so he could zip up his jacket and wrap his plaid scarf around his neck. He was always getting colds, if not full-blown flus, and because of this he always wanted to keep his neck warm. He could stand frozen ears and fingers. And toes. But he wanted it to be nice and toasty where he swallowed.

Across the street, would-be theatergoers were waiting at

the half-price ticket booth, waiting, Val thought, like the pigeons that waddled close to them, dreaming of a handout, a kernel or two of something flung at them. Well, he guessed they wouldn't be getting tickets to the Palace tonight. It had a hit on its hands. He'd heard that scalpers were getting two hundred bucks apiece for seats in the back row of the orchestra. He forced himself to turn around and confront the poster, confront the glossy yet bloodless lips of the drag queens from *La Cage aux Folles II*. He chuckled to himself, then picked up his paper bag and moved down Broadway towards Times Square. Just south of Seventh and Forty-Second Street was his favorite Irish bar where Benny, its friendly bartender, mixed the stiffest gin and tonics in midtown.

"How's your arthritis?" Val asked as he slipped onto a stool.

"I can still pick up ice cubes," Benny snorted, wiping the space clean in front of Val. The dampness the towel left picked up the slant of the October sun. "A double?"

"Please, Benny."

The only other customer was a black man at the far end of the bar who seemed engrossed in the football game on the cable TV. Val lit a cigarette and tried to focus on the game, but the same ray of sun that shone on the bar obliterated the screen so Val had to give up. "Guess it's just that time of day," he remarked, blowing smoke rings toward the mirrored lineup of liquor bottles, but neither the black guy nor Benny acknowledged that he had said anything.

Benny leaned against the cash register, polishing whiskey

glasses, meticulously checking for spots. Val found this incongruous since Benny's apron was covered with grease stains. He slowly sipped his drink.

"How's your brother these days?" Benny broke the silence.

"Ray?" Val's eyes lit up. "Fine, fine."

"What happened with his suit?"

"They paid up. Five grand." Last winter, Ray, leaving the McDonald's he managed in midtown, had fallen in front of a department store on a section of ice that should have been shoveled. Ray sued for negligence, insisting he had hurt his back, and won his case, even though he couldn't get a doctor to write a letter substantiating the injury. "But they sure gave poor Ray a time of it. Bastards. Didn't offer him nothin'. He had to bleed it out of them, so to speak. He was laid up around the house a couple of months. Fran — you know — his ex . . . she never called or came over once. He only had me to look after him."

Val remembered with irritation those long winter evenings when he would leave his job as a bookkeeper in an export company in the Garment District and board the Staten Island ferry back to the modest house in South Beach his parents had willed to him and his brother. After a bus ride from the ferry, and a walk to get supplies, he would come in around eight PM to find his brother in bed, watching TV, popping aspirin after aspirin, swearing his head off, trying to ease his back into a comfortable position.

It had been Ray who had split the house two ways, living, at least up until a year ago, with his wife, Fran, in the lower half while Val had the upstairs, complete with hot plate and refrigerator, to himself. Now, after Ray's divorce and accident, Val found himself being invited down to share a meal or watch a TV show with Ray. Val was thirty-five; Ray, thirty-nine. As long as Val could remember, his older brother had guided him along life's path, and silently, lazily, they had always stuck together.

Suddenly Val broke into a hacking cough and angrily stubbed the remainder of his cigarette in the ashtray. "Went right to my throat, just where I didn't want it to go." He took a gulp of gin. "I'm gonna give these damn things up."

Benny patted him on the shoulder and grinned. "I quit — let's see — about seven years ago. You'll find it's easier than you think."

"Yeah."

"But, Val, you're looking real good, buddy. More relaxed than I've seen you in a long time. You don't have those deep lines on your forehead anymore."

"That's my think tank up there. It's gotta have a few creases to show the parts are still working."

Benny laughed. "They're still working. You knew enough to come back to my joint, didn't you?"

"See that?" Val moved his finger around the rim of his glass. Suddenly a dreamy vision came floating before his eyes . . . bright red clouds . . . glittering sunshine . . . plumes . . .

Unexpectedly, the reverie came into focus like a blurred piece of film a projectionist makes sharp. It was the *La Cage aux Folles II* poster he had stared at this afternoon, the red clouds the dresses of the drag queens whose brazen eyes attached themselves to his own. He quickly checked his watch. Only a little after four. With brisk determination, he crossed to the pay phone in the corner and called Beth.

"Hello?" she answered tentatively after seven rings.

"It's me."

"Who is it? Val?"

"Sure. Don't you recognize my voice?"

"Of course I do. I guessed it was you, didn't I?"

"You didn't sound positive."

"Well, no harm done. What's on your mind?"

"I've got a couple of hours to kill. I thought you might like some company."

"Right now?"

"I can be there in twenty minutes."

"Well . . . OK."

"See you then." Val returned to the bar where he downed the last of his drink.

Benny gave him a quizzical look. "What was that all about?"

"A girl I've been seeing."

"Lucky stiff."

"I think so." He pressed a five-dollar bill into Benny's hand. "Keep the change." Then, picking up his paper bag and bundling his scarf around his neck, he walked through the revolving door into the heart of Times Square.

"They're tiger lilies," she said. "Aren't they gorgeous?"

Val had to admit they were. The proud, ferocious buds dominated the small room, set as they were on the round

93

birch table, its circumference so wide you had to maneuver yourself around it to get from one end of the room to the other. On the south end was an open kitchen, its recently washed-down cabinets stained with mildew. At the north end a single bed was pushed up against the wall. Next to it was a door which led into a bathroom barely big enough to hold the sink, shower stall, and toilet. The studio's two windows faced the tenement across the street. It was the table that seemed to be the center of Beth's life.

Val stared at the lilies. "Where'd you get 'em?"

Beth blushed very slightly. "Never mind."

"Oh, I get it. A present." He added contritely, "I guess I should have brought you something."

"No, Val."

"What would you like, so I'll remember for next time. A bracelet? Some little gold earrings? I saw a guy hawking some on my way over. They looked pretty OK."

"You don't have to get me anything."

"But I want to, Beth, I want to."

"Well, then surprise me with something next time." Beth rearranged some of the lilies, glad to have a task at hand so she could turn away from Val's intensity which usually unnerved her. Everything she said he seemed to pick apart for no reason.

"Wallpaper's getting a little tatty."

"Tell Gus. That's not my problem."

"Hey, look," Val said. "Do you have some mouthwash? I've been drinking gin, oh, don't worry, just one, but my breath stinks like the bottom of the bottle."

"It's OK. Forget about it."

Val fidgeted, hands in pocket.

"There's some in the bathroom cabinet," Beth said as she began to undo her blouse, realizing it would prey on his mind.

Val gargled, wondering if the minty taste would suit Beth. Hell, maybe she didn't care. But he wanted her to care.

When he came out of the bathroom she was lying across the bed in just her panties, her breasts meager, her skin taut with an almost unattractive crispness, like parchment. She had the body of a little girl, but she was aging. What still kept her desirable was her unassuming vulnerability.

Val took thirty bucks out of his wallet.

"Never mind the money, Val. I know you're kind of strapped right now because of Ray and all."

"No. I pay for what ain't mine." He dropped the bills on the bureau.

He and Beth Jackson had grown up in the same neighborhood, played together sometimes, had taken notice of each other as they passed puberty. Val had always been a little heartsick for Beth, especially when she worked as a grocery check-out girl in the South Beach shopping mall, trying to support herself at sixteen. It was during that time that Gus had come along, a pimp who worked the lower-class districts of Staten Island and shipped what young meat he could sweet-talk into Manhattan.

It had worked like a charm for Beth, these last eighteen years. Gus had set her up in her West Forty-Seventh Street apartment between Ninth and Tenth avenues. Her small world on the large island of Manhattan was plenty and the eighteen years seemed like one.

Gus had lifted every emotional and financial burden from her shoulders. Val liked it that way, too. When he found out where she was and what she did, the inhibitions he had harbored before disappeared. He could take her for a price without embarrassment and without being judged. And all on his terms. He watched her now, waiting for him. He slowly sat on a chair and carefully removed his shoes. "You don't mind if I keep my socks on?"

"No, of course not."

"No use catching a cold."

"You don't have to worry. It's warm in here."

He stood and slipped off his suspenders and trousers and laid them over the back of the chair.

"How have you been, Val? How's South Beach?"

"Fine, fine. It's a long way back there for you now, isn't it?"

"An ocean away," she laughed.

He removed his shirt, then his boxer shorts and T-shirt, before settling on the edge of the bed. "Take your panties off."

"Yes, Val." She inched them down around her ankles then flicked them to the floor with her foot. "What do you want to do this afternoon?"

"Let's eat each other up."

After they had both climaxed, Val, taking off the pillowcase and wrapping it around his neck, apologized, "I'm afraid I wasn't very good this afternoon."

"You were just fine."

"Don't lie. Just because you got paid doesn't mean you have to lie."

"I wasn't — "

"God, I wish I had a cigarette, but I gave them up."

"I didn't know that."

"Yeah, this afternoon at Benny's I decided to call it quits. Anyway, sorry I wasn't good today but my mind was on my mission."

"What mission?"

"Serious business. Real serious. Anyway, it'll be better next time." Val glanced at his watch. "Five-thirty." He dressed and washed his face and hands then sat back in the chair. "You don't mind if I wait here, do you, just for a little bit? You ain't expecting a guy, are you?"

"Not for a while." Beth draped a robe around her shoulders and looked down to the street. "Crazy how it starts to get dark so soon."

"I like that. You just said something that's gonna be true for a lot of pansies tonight. It's gonna be dark for them . . ."

"What do you mean 'dark'?"

"Look in my paper bag. Don't touch anything. Just kind of lean over and peek inside."

Beth did as instructed but couldn't recognize the contents. "What is it?"

"They're pipe bombs. I have 'em wired to go off at eight-fifteen."

"What are you talking about?"

"I'm planting them in the theater down the street that has a big fag show going on. There's gonna be some fireworks tonight. Real ones. They won't be coming from the stage."

"Hah-hah."

"I ain't kidding."

"You are so."

"I'm dead serious, Beth. I'm up to here with these fuckin' fags running over this town like rats, a bunch of titless women spreading their sick diseases that could contaminate the whole city."

"You just like to talk. You wouldn't do something so nuts."

"Oh, wouldn't I? Just wait and see. I've been thinking about it for a long time."

"What do you have against queers anyway?" Beth straightened his collar. "I mean, personally. You're always down on them."

"I hate their pussies, that's why. Half the problems in this town can be laid right down at their feet."

"But I mean, what did they ever do to you?"

He pulled her down onto his lap. "They exist. That's enough." He nibbled on her ear.

"Stop!" She pulled away, giggling. "I don't believe you could hate them so much without them having tried anything with you."

"Well, I'll tell you, Beth. Remember that old shack down on Cleary Street by the beach, the one they used to store buoys and lifeboats in?"

"I think so."

"Well, there was this old guy who used to hang around there, pretending to be a security man. One summer day he got my brother. Flashed a badge and ordered Ray inside and got him up the ass. Ray came home crying and told me all about it. Later some of Ray's friends got buggered by the same guy. Same place, same modus operandi. We found out who he was. Retired post office employee. He and his wife lived up on Maple Court. Ray and me had always been good with firecrackers — we'd set 'em off all summer long — so we tossed a few good ones at old man Bowman's house. Then we called Bowman and his wife and told them to get out of the neighborhood or we'd blow their house up. We were just kids, only eleven or twelve, but we scared 'em off."

"Funny . . . I sort of remember them. Her at least. Pulling her shopping trolley up the hill."

"I thought you'd come around. A few years later we blew up the shack on the beach. Needless to say, all memories of Bowman were erased."

"Not all memories, Val." Beth stood up, agitated.

"So you still don't believe those bombs are in there?"

"I can't believe it."

"They are, and before the night is over, they'll have to put fresh wings on more than a couple of fairies."

"But if you set off bombs in a theater, it'll kill other people, not just the queers."

"Then they deserve it for being queer-lovers." He smiled, relishing the thought of women rushing up the aisles, their evening dresses in flames, their faces caked with blood. "Next time the queers put on a show, people will think twice before going."

"You've always liked to pull my leg. Always. When we were kids you'd make up the craziest stories and get me to believe them. I'd start to cry and then you'd laugh and tell me it was all a joke . . ." She had moved quietly to the paper bag and once more tried to look down inside, but this time with a desperate need to know what it contained. But all she saw were black shadows on layered sheets.

"They say it's a sin, but no one bothers to punish them. The preachers on TV — "

"They would say what we just did was wrong," Beth argued.

"They don't care about that. I'm sure half of 'em visit girls like you on the side. It's the queers they hate."

It's the queers they hate. Girls like you on the side. On the side. Beth's head was spinning. She tried to steady herself against the table. Her eyes pressed against the lilies and their blue veins seemed like welcome rivers coursing through an orange hell. She felt his hands pressing onto her shoulders. "I love you, Beth. That's why I've shared my secret with you and only you. It's our secret. It's something we'll share — just you and me — till the end of time." *It's our secret. Till the end of time.*

Val lifted the vase of tiger lilies from the table. "I need these. I'll pay you for them."

Suddenly she broke out in laughter. "Why in the world? You'll pay me for them? All right, then, leave me a million dollars." But he was gone from the room taking both the flowers and the paper bag with him.

Once again Val found himself in the entryway of the Palace Theater, but this time the middle doors to the lobby swung open at the touch of his hand.

"What do you want?" an older woman in a rumpled usher's outfit asked him.

"A delivery."

"Who for?"

"The stage manager."

"Those flowers?"

"Yeah."

She sighed impatiently. "You have to take 'em around to the stage door."

"It's locked," he lied. "The guard told me to bring them through the lobby."

"Well, as long as I don't have to take them. I'm in the middle of my program count."

"Don't bother yourself."

"Wait." She put her hand on Val's arm and, huffing, explained, "You have to go up on the stage and down the left corridor till you come to a big cluster of trunks crammed with costumes. His office is right behind them."

Val moved on into the theater, surprised that it was so brightly lit; he had imagined he'd be getting the protection of a dark house, but the only shadowy spot was the stage itself. He would have to keep moving, to appear as if he belonged there, to avoid suspicion. He didn't think that would be too hard. He had always come across as average, had never turned heads.

With a light step he approached the stage, looking down either side of the aisle at the long rows of seats, hoping to find the perfect spot for one of his bombs. But there was no secure place; it would be discovered before the show started if he put it under a seat.

The stage rose before him, dim and unfriendly, almost challenging him to try to do it harm. The orchestra pit was now at arm's length — here there had to be a dark corner, maybe at the edge of the pit itself, behind part of the black curtain that was draped all around. But he didn't want to kill members of the orchestra when he could go after real fag meat on the stage. And before he knew it, he was up there, looking out into the empty theater.

Nobody was on to him. A few ushers at the back of the house were talking among themselves. On either side of him, in the wings, stagehands were busy putting scenery on rollers.

On the stage, a set was already mantled. He could make out palm trees and a vista of white clouds and blue skies. Tables set along a promenade, and on the low sea wall a row of potted flowers. A stroke of unexpected luck. The tiger lilies would not only serve as his ticket of admission but as his calling card as well. He set the vase on the wall, between two gardenia bushes, then knelt down and carefully removed one of the bombs from his paper bag and eased it down into the vase.

But where to put the other? The balcony jutted out invitingly. He wound up the stairs to the right of the orchestra and entered the gallery. Down below, bits of the set swam vaguely before him — here a cloud, here a chair, here a painted wave. If only the bomb would explode first on the stage, then seconds later, while people were screaming or in shock, up here. His eyes scanned the balcony, up and down, back and forth. Nothing but rows of empty seats. Discouraged, he headed through the curtain to the area outside the lounges.

He spotted it immediately, the water fountain in a tall marble nave. He planted the second bomb down behind its shiny cavity against the wall. It was completely hidden.

An effeminate young usher rounded the top of the stairs. He stopped, a little surprised, and blinked at Val. Val felt a terrible wrath building. He crumpled his empty paper bag into a small wad and dropped it into a trash bin. Then he headed to the stairs. He paused on the first step down and glared at the usher who held a flashlight in one hand and a stack of playbills in the other.

"Know what you can do with that flashlight?" Val asked. "Shove it way up your ass, fruit fly!"

The usher laughed nervously at first, but then turned and walked swiftly towards the lounge, licking his wounds.

She had locked herself in the Howard Johnson's Ladies and was snorting coke off a ten-dollar bill. That stupid Val. She had been an ass to let him get her goat. He was full of shit, way up to his eyes. He was a joker. A sick joker who always messed her head up. Well, she wouldn't believe anything he said anymore. Not only that, she would never even listen to it.

A knock on the door.

"One minute," she called out as she finished her snort. She could feel the hit now, that familiar euphoria rushing through her body. She stuffed the bill in her purse and opened the door on some short, blue-haired old broad, probably some tourist from the Americana across the street. Well, she reasoned, *thank God for tourists who give me bread. And trespass against me.* The men from out of town were often around Broadway at this hour, coming back to their hotels after business meetings, before going to dinner and maybe the theater or a movie. Maybe not, if she could persuade them otherwise.

She had worn her light green halter top even though it was chilly, and she sat in her accustomed spot at the counter by the window exactly as Gus had taught her to do. She was to sip a strawberry soda with her eyes fixed on the men in business suits outside. She was to create a picture of girlish innocence and yet of secret abilities at the same time. And she was not to get thrown out by the management. If a man returned her stare, she was to put her money down on the counter and go outside to him.

"Hi, Beth," Darlene called out. "The usual?"

"The usual." Coke and a soda. Coke and ice cream. Whatever you called it, it was a nice combination. Her glazed eyes searched for men through the window. No one looked in. Except a man in rags who was talking to himself. Beth lowered her eyes.

Darlene put the strawberry soda down in front of her. "I put in three scoops for you tonight. Looks like you could stand some more meat on your bones."

"Thanks."

"How've you been, lamb?"

"Can't complain."

"You serious?" Darlene peered down at her over horn-rimmed glasses. "Then you're a very lucky girl."

"Maybe I am, in a lot of ways."

"Got a secret billionaire lover I don't know about?" She had a delivery like a regular on a sitcom. "Some guy who's gonna whisk you up in a fancy limousine?"

"No, just Gus."

"Oh, Gus is the fellow's name, huh? What's this Gus like? You and him been goin' together a long time?"

"Yeah. He saved my life." And the moment when he'd first appeared before her came back very suddenly. She had just finished ringing up some groceries when a hand shot out of nowhere and covered hers. "I saw you stealing," he had said. It was only much later that she had found out that that was his opening line to nearly every teenage girl who worked behind a cash register in South Beach, for more often than not they had pilfered at one time or another at least a quarter if not more. She had trembled, since she had stolen five dollars a week ago and felt that he had spotted her. "We'll talk about it after you get off work." And he had been waiting for her in his van and she had sidled in next to him and he had immediately put her at ease.

They drove down by the ferry terminal and he insisted on taking her then and there. And her a virgin. She would always remember the back of his van, the paintings of wild animals, striped zebras, tigers, wild deer, all under purple light, and she and Gus lying on a thick piece of purple carpet. Gus looked then as he did now, a tall man with shoulder-length curly hair and an earring in his left ear. He smelled like bubble bath and had a kind smile.

She had clung to him. And by midnight she had agreed to give up her life for his, even though he made her understand that there were to be many men afterwards, so many she would lose count in just a short time. "My hand trembled under his."

"What?" Darlene mumbled as she filled the salt shakers. "Oh, yeah, your Gus."

"He saved me from a miserable existence." Her eyes went to the street. Dozens of men, now, passing by, but she was looking right through them. She felt like slapping herself. Concentrate. She must concentrate. But the coke had made her feel she was seeing past everything, right up to the sunset over the Pacific.

"Somebody's staring at you," Darlene commented matter-of-factly.

He was better-than-average looking, about forty-five, wearing a white Stetson hat and a grey suit. He was grinning at her.

"I've got to go." She jumped off the stool and thrust a dollar into Darlene's hands.

Taxis zigzagged by, delivering theatergoers, but in between honks he purred, "You sure are a pretty girl. I couldn't help noticing you. What's your name?"

"Beth."

"Now I haven't heard that name for a long time. It's about as pretty as you are. My name's Mike Green. I'm from Lexington, Kentucky. Ever been down that way?"

She shook her head.

"No, of course not. You're a New Yorker through and through. Anyone could tell that."

She smiled.

"You're one of these New Yorkers that think it all ends over there at the Hudson River. Nothing beyond that. You didn't even ask me if I had something to do with racing, seeing I'm from Lexington. Don't you like horses?"

"I've never been around any," she mumbled sweetly.

"Well, I can't help you out there," he laughed. "I'm in insurance. I could be from Anywhere, U.S.A."

"Are you staying in a hotel in the area?" Beth came to the point.

"Yeah." He followed her lead. "But in the same room as my son. I just brought him into the company this year. It's his first trip East. He's out drinking with some guys from the New York office." He gave Beth a wink. "I'm too old to enjoy that kind of thing. I thought I'd do some exploring instead. See if there was anything new in town."

"Well . . . I have a place just down the street." Jittery, she moved from one foot to the other.

"You're some lady. I thought you might be waiting for your boyfriend the way you were poised up there on the counter sipping your soda."

"Would you like to stop by?"

"I guess you weren't waiting for your boyfriend . . . Sure, why not?"

She nodded with relief and started briskly down Forty-Seventh Street, silently taking Mike by the arm. Cold, she increased their pace, glancing away from the Broadway lights which glittered strongly tonight through the crystal clear autumn air. She liked it better when it rained. Rain to her was the sweetest sound on earth, rain on the pavement, on the roofs of cars, on leaves of trees, and the rain and mist always toned down the bright neon hanging wherever she walked.

He had rushed to the ferry, having wanted to get back home in time for the ten o'clock news. Well, he would definitely be on time as it was only eight o'clock now. Though calmer than a cucumber when he had planted the bombs, he now felt queasy with only a few minutes to go till they would explode.

He found a seat on the outside deck. He needed the air even if it meant he might catch cold. He wrapped himself up as best he could, snuggling down into his coat and pulling his cap over his ears, watching the Brooklyn skyline as the boat moved south on the blackened water. He couldn't wait for Ray's reaction when he saw the report on the news that a bunch of faggots had had their guts blown out. No doubt he'd jump around the room like a fucking madman and open one of the bottles of champagne they kept under the floorboards in the basement, and after they had drained the last drop, Val would tell him that he'd been the one who did it.

"Fuckin' no!"

"Yeah, Ray, it was me, I did it."

"Don't shit me, now. I've had too much damn champagne."

"I swear to God. I did it."

"Oh, no. I don't believe it. Swear."

"I do."

"Swear on this fucking bottle of champagne."

"I swear it."

"Swear on the day we sent Bowman's little beach shack all the way to hell."

"I swear it."

"Then you have really passed through the flames, brother. You know, Val, I've never really thought of you as a man before — you've only been a kid brother — but now you've — "

Like a sudden storm, four or five kids ran down the deck, yelling and screaming. Val swayed like a balloon, forgetting who and where he was. With some effort, he regained his equilibrium. Now what had his brother been saying to him? Oh, yes. "You've only been a kid brother — but now you've . . . you've . . . you've . . ."

"Not much to look at," Mike's appraisal was blunt, not hiding his disappointment.

"This afternoon I had some beautiful tiger lilies in here." Beth locked the door behind them and she escorted Mike around the table. "Sorry you weren't here earlier. You can sit down on the bed."

"Where are you going to plant yourself?" He was appalled that there were only a couple of wooden chairs and no sofa.

"I'll fix us something to drink. What would you like?"

"What I'd like is an ashtray, if you have one. I'd like to smoke a cigarette."

Beth edged her way around the table into the kitchen. "Reach your hand under the bed. Down by your foot."

Mike's fingers felt under the fringe of the bedspread. He pulled out an ashtray that held a few butts. "You want a cigarette too?" he asked, lighting up.

"No," she said quickly as she dropped ice cubes in a glass. "I don't smoke."

Then the butts were from her tricks. *High class joint*, Mike thought, suddenly depressed.

"What did you say you wanted to drink?" She was nervous tonight. She didn't know why but she didn't want to focus in on anything.

"Scotch on the rocks?" Mike suggested.

Like a somnambulist, she brought a bottle of Scotch out of the cabinet and poured it to the top of the glass. Then she approached him, holding it as if she were bringing a glass of milk to a sick child.

He took it from her. "I'll just set it down here on the floor," he said cheerfully. "You know, I was out in Phoenix last year. Do they have some top-notch whorehouses, let me tell you."

She folded her arms and laughed softly, encouragingly.

"I went to this really classy place. Spotless. Beautiful women. The rooms had luxury whirlpools, baths, open bars, every amenity, you name it, they had it. I was with this dark-haired lady called Lacey. We were on one of these beds that rotate real slow in a circle. It was the goddamnedest thing I'd ever seen. Imagine a bed that turns 360 degrees while you're going to town on it. And a big mirror on the ceiling so you can watch yourselves ball. Now that, that was a night to remember." Sighing, he stubbed out his cigarette and lowered his eyes. "I kissed Lacey all over her lovely body hundreds of times before . . . it was over. I kissed the insides of her thighs, her breasts, her hands — "

My trembling hands. Gus, did you save my life? Then where is the proof? You brought me here to perform. And I have. I have. Then where is my reward?

"Oh, well, that was then . . ." He put his hands on her waist. "This is now. How much?"

"Fifty?"

"That's cheap . . ." His affability was on the wane now. "Why don't you show me your stuff? I can't stay too long. I have to get back to the hotel, shower and go out to dinner with my son."

When she was naked, he pulled her down on top of him. He had unbuttoned his fly and now he entered her, without bothering to strip. For a while he rode her as she straddled him, then he shoved her back onto the bed, climbed on top of her and thrust harder and deeper, biting her nipples, becoming more excited.

Beth was his docile plaything, but her mind was her own and inside it was a vision, a private apparition. She was stepping out of the darkness into light and she was throwing bouquets of flowers forward. When one bunch was gone another appeared in her hand. From thin air. Marigolds, chrysanthemums, gladiolas. She cast them all before her. Was she on a stage? How could she be? She was no actress. And she'd never even been to the theater . . . Ah, no. She saw suddenly where she was. She was not standing on a stage but on the head of a giant pin which was tottering somewhere in space.

"Wait!" She suddenly dug her nails into Mike's shoulders. "Stop a minute . . ."

"Why?" he asked, his voice hoarse.

"I thought I heard an explosion."

"What?"

"In the distance . . . I heard two explosions, one right after the other."

"No . . . no . . ." he said impatiently. "You didn't hear any-thing . . ."

HALLOWEEN CARD

THE PARTY WAS AT THE FISHOFF LOFT, A WOEBEGOTTEN, cobwebbed space south of Soho. It was once, probably not that long ago, a garment sweatshop. And Reb Fishoff had turned this slice of the past into his own conceit — among his sculptures stood rusty old workbenches and, on the floor beneath them, dress scraps half turned to dust. Reb had refused to tear down the walls and incorporate the adjoining employees' washroom, damp with mould, with its long row of toilet stalls, into the loft proper, even though it would have increased his work area by a third. Ghostly mirrors, cracked and perfect for the party, still hung over the bathroom sinks, and as Reb spotted them with rubber spiders, he swore he could see the dim figures of the garment workers float close and roll up their sleeves, anxious to wash their exhausted fingers. He avoided their eyes. His fingers were exhausted too, but from his own pleasure, from forming the reedy, human-like sculptures that were his life.

Glancing into the street below, he caught glimpses of trick-or-treaters hurrying past shut groceries and warehouses toward the well-lit neighborhood to the west. He adjusted the clasp on his mad wolf's costume and fingered the hideous mask that would soon obscure his eccentric good looks. Eccentric? That brought a smile to his lips, but only a slight smile. The clock in the store across the street was a pink neon

115

moon. Only an hour till party time.

"Miguelito," Jane Wilson commanded softly as she added the finishing touches to her cat face, "put something on the record player."

"What?"

"Oh, anything . . . No, not anything. Put on Gershwin. *Rhapsody in Blue.*"

"Jane," Michael Iacca groaned; it was already becoming stifling in his Pan outfit. "There's no time for the *Rhapsody . . .*"

"Oh, all right. Then put on Edith Sitwell reading that long poem . . . or is it a play?" She lost her train of thought as she concentrated on brushing her upper lip with briar red gloss. The crash of the jazz symphony stunned her. "*Miguelito*, I thought you said there was no time for the *Rhapsody!*"

"Oh, cut the crap. There'll be enough witches at the party, I don't want to hear another one murder her own poetry." He lit a fat joint and like a footman carried it to her.

Jane stood and regarded herself critically in the mirror. Her silver-grey gown clung to her all the way down, until it swept the floor. Michael, his boyish face wizened, wiggled his cloven foot in approval. A full shoulder shorter than Jane anyway, now crouched and playing on his pipe, his red hair bursting through the glossy green head paint, he cut a meek figure.

"I could squash you — like an ant!" Jane laughed, and her laugh was as silver and tight as her gown.

They swayed in front of the mirror to the bluesy horns and

piano.

"Don't you think I make a fetching pussy?" Jane took a deep drag on the joint. "I'm just glossing my top lip. Nothing on the bottom."

"I hope Reb has asked some hot guys this time," Michael stopped cavorting and paused, winded.

"I do, too. But then, he usually does, doesn't he?"

Cinderella approached the candlelit mirror — coyly for someone speeding. Pinpoints of light flashed around her crown, and her eyes kept crossing and uncrossing and moving forward into the mirror then back again. She approved of the braided blonde locks that rested on her bare shoulders even though it was a stiff wig she'd bought for a buck and her ball gown was made from dreams. She rummaged through her evening bag, counting enough cash to get her to and from the party by taxi.

The weather report was on the radio. Dracula listened as he lay in his hammock, attaching his killer fingernails with care and expertise. Sinking below freezing tonight. Frost on the pumpkin. He'd need his cape indeed. Purple and shining on the metal coatrack. The same silky material as the hammock he was lounging on. Enveloped in sin. Like he'd been all summer long when he'd quit his job and gone out to the Hamptons where the girls in the beach house had served him. He'd swung on the hammock and let the fresh sun sting him all over his body, inch by inch. Slow. *Ouch. Fake fingernail meets tender flesh. Draws blood. Where is the expertise now? Where was it then, as the summer waned and the nights grew cold? Why did that same sea turn frigid and violent so that he couldn't recognize it anymore?* Now, all alone in his basement studio, he listened to the weather, and the past and present formed a clot in his ear like a shell. He finished lacquering on the last nail and scratched against the window to try to frighten the two little boys outside rummaging through their sacks of candy.

The Halloween cards read:

GHASTLY FEST. REB FISHOFF. MIDNIGHT UNTIL. BY INVITATION ONLY. AND ONLY YOU KNOW WHERE.

Jane and Michael studied theirs as they hailed a cab. "Surely we don't have to carry these," Jane whined.

"Naturally not." Michael ripped his in two. "Reb would know us anywhere." He dropped the two pieces of paper into the breeze, and they laughed as one piece plummeted to the gutter while the other was sucked up into the blackness.

Skulls that glow in the dark. Drunken floozies. Supermen. Creatures - fine representatives from the animal, mineral and vegetable kingdoms. A man with a sensual cream torso and a vulture's head poured over a deck of Tarot cards scattered blithely over a Monopoly board balancing on the heater.

Dracula, sitting back on the bumpy couch, watched the

118

partygoers spin before him like the colors dripping down a wax candle in the dead of night. A cat tried to lick goo off the fake dreadful fingernails. Dracula shooed him away. *It's hot in here and the party is almost ready to become boring. But not quite yet. The make-up has to finish dripping and the rest of the liquor has to be consumed and all the drugs have to start wearing off.*

It was cooler in the bathroom. And more brightly lit. Jane sat before the mirror reapplying her lip gloss. A couple of guys came in and peed in the stalls. Jane was amused: they didn't bother to close the doors. She couldn't tell who they were anyway. Cinderella was beside her, adjusting her crown. Jane didn't recognize her. She noticed that Cinderella was sweaty and that her eyes were watery. Jane started to leave. But Cinderella held her back. She pinched her arm.

"What is it?" Jane asked, startled.

Cinderella's touch was cold and clammy. Suddenly Jane was shoved into one of the stalls, and Cinderella forced her back down against the toilet as she latched the door behind them. As a hand was slipped over her mouth, Jane realized that Cinderella was a man. Very clever disguise, she thought, not quite afraid. The man tore at her dress. Jane feebly tried to push the masquerader back, but she was so stoned that she gave up. She would have almost let King Kong fuck her. If there was someone more freaked than she was, it was the man trying to have sex with her. His movements were so halted and drawn out. He wore blue jeans under his gown, and he unzipped them like a nurse fastidiously pulling down a bandage to see if the wound is OK. Finally his cock was ready to go in. She saw Michael through the space in the stall door, framed by the dirty mirror on one side and the big blonde locks of the man above her on the other. Michael was half here, half there, yet ultimately far away in time. He needn't look for her. "I'm not being raped," she whispered. "It's only Halloween. And I don't think he entered me successfully." Michael disappeared. *"Miguelito . . . did you find any man you like? . . . Did you see the one in the corner, dressed as a bat? . . . There was a bulge down there you would have liked . . . oh, Miguelito . . . let's go back home . . . Did you see the man dressed as the devil? . . . you would have loved his thick red mustache . . . and his hands seemed so strong."* Cinderella collapsed before her and his head dropped back against the door. Jane stood and pulled down her dress. The man shot her a surprised glance, jumped up, pulled back the latch and rushed from the room, his gown tucked up over his jeans. Jane could only laugh.

"Do you see them, too?"

Jane whirled around to face the seedy-eyed wolf.

"Oh, Reb, you frightened me. Do I see what?"

"Just now you were laughing. I thought you might have seen the garment workers in the mirror. I invited them as well. They're here too, dancing with us. They need to laugh and have a good time like we're having. Their ghosts need a little relaxation."

"I don't know what the fuck you're talking about. I was laughing because I just had a rather pathetic, unsexy encounter with a man in one of these stalls. A creature dressed as Cinderella who was obviously so high — "

"You know, this is a funky party." Reb pulled off his wolf's head. He stared at her impatiently with his violet eyes. "It's not a rich man's bash like some of the ones uptown. Black tie and suspenders. Highest grade coke. Highest grade trash." He smiled gently. "This is a party for poor *artistes*."

"Who was that guy?"

Reb began to laugh. "You're so stoned. Your words are all jumbled."

"Don't make fun of me! Who was that guy all dolled up in that blonde wig and fancy dress! I just may want to press charges against him when I'm sober!" Her lips quivered, and Reb could see she was surprised at the intensity in her own voice.

"Gee, I don't know, Jane. I really don't. Let's go see if we can find him."

They searched the loft, but the culprit wasn't to be found. Michael was talking to an old man in a wizard's tunic who held a long staff with a sparkling purple stone imbedded on its top. Jane became mesmerized by the stone and she dropped her head on Michael's shoulder. "Miguelito . . ." she whispered. Michael laughed and gently eased her away. She slipped down against the window. There on the other side of the street was the man dressed as Cinderella, running west, fighting the wind. "There!" she screamed excitedly and pulled Reb down to her. "There he goes!"

"Sugar-pussy, I have no idea who it is!" he laughed. "Why don't you relax and have a good time now?"

She giggled in spite of herself. "You're right, I'm being too serious."

"Drink some more. Get really stoned. You can crash here if you like. It is Halloween."

"And let some evil beasty try and get me again?"

But Reb was off, his eyes on the silk-chested vulture divining futures.

Jane was back in the bathroom in front of the mirror around four AM. A chill was in the air, and her hand was shaking as she raised her lip gloss towards her mouth. For some reason she paused. Out of the corner of her eye she saw a tiger twisting in the corner, a set of headphones covering his ears. Suddenly she was annoyed. *Every cliché in the book* . . . Impulsively, in an angry scrawl she wrote, *Fuck you, Reb, You Laid One Lousy Party on a Bunch of Friends. We'd have been better off uptown at a* . . . The last letters were big and formless and almost unreadable . . . she was nearly asleep. Suddenly the lip gloss was removed from her hand, and a fingernail brushed against her cheek. Dracula stood beside her. "What do you know about uptown parties?" He ran a red line through her carelessly written message. "Don't bother, Jane." He dropped the lip gloss on the floor and ground it into the tiles with his boot. "Feel my banana."

"Don't be silly."

"No, really, baby."

Jane considered lightly rubbing against the man's groin but stopped herself. Dracula whipped out a real bona fide banana from behind his back. "Pinched it off Carmen Miranda in there. And I have the nails to peel it with." *Laughter. Nails. Play-acting. But soon enough real coffins. And the loss of time.* Jane slumped against the masquerader who raised her up and gently guided her into the stall and pulled the door shut behind them.

"Jane, it's Grace Ford."

"Grace, I haven't seen you in ages. And no wonder I didn't recognize you. You were gone all summer long, weren't you?"

"I was in the Hamptons with Barbara Koonz and her gang. I lay in the hammock and listened to the sea . . . Sometimes I fantasized about you, Jane, although I knew you weren't a lesbian."

"Not a lesbian?" Her voice drifted. Her eyes closed and she could hear Grace biting hurriedly at her fingernails. *I want to get these damn things off.* Then she felt Grace's finger playing around the edges of her pussy. How the finger got there so quickly, she didn't know. But she liked it. Grace was young and beautiful, wasn't she? And kind and clever? Jane wanted to be held. Opening her eyes, she saw Michael through the space in the door. He was framed by a long fingernail on Grace's right hand and a distant form lost in the mirror behind him. *"Miguelito . . . who is dancing from so long ago? Don't you see? Behind you in the mirror? Hurry . . . that figure . . . so grey and sad?"* Grace's lips kissed hers. *"Miguelito . . . I am here . . . always here . . ."* The dim dancer vanished, and Michael gazed at the door of the stall, perplexed. *"Yes, I am here . . . here . . . did you see the one dressed as the Ugly Duckling? Nothing ugly about him underneath, you understand? Didn't you recognize him, darling? . . . It was Kevin, the one you had a crush on last summer . . . Did you see the one who's reading the Tarot? If I know you, he's driving you out of your mind! Isn't he? Isn't he, Miguelito?"*

The next thing Jane remembered was waking up, gradually. She was sitting on the window ledge, and Reb was in front of her, a frown on his face. He was looking past her into the night and he was shaking slightly. The guests were oblivious to whatever seemed to concern him and they continued to sweep around the loft, dancing. Jane slowly turned and followed Reb's gaze. She gasped. Coming towards them was a giant cyclone, ripping through the streets of Manhattan with the fierceness of Hell.

"A twister." Reb's throat was so dry the words hardly came. Jane grabbed his hand.

The room turned a ghastly yellow. Everybody stood still, afraid. Then the wind struck. The incredible force was unleashed — everything was spinning and suspended and upside down. And everyone was screaming. But soon the screams were lost as in a dream and Hell itself became pleasant and they felt only like laundry flapping, sheets brushing against each other in a warm breeze. Then there was the thud and they crashed to the floor. And all the movement stopped.

There was the sound of birds. And the stream of dawn. And the smell of hay and dying grass.

Jane pulled herself to the window. Outside were fields of faded wheat limpid with dew and apple trees that climbed beside telephone poles into the long, flat distance.

"God knows where we are." She turned to the others who were looking around with shocked, panicky faces.

They voted to crawl through the window one by one and

then gather as a pack and explore. Their costumes lit the dull morning, and the birds, seemingly jealous, flew in circles above their heads, squawking. The noise roused some farmers from a nearby house who came out on the porch, rifles in hand, their grim faces fixed on the intruders. Jane began walking forward and others followed, some breaking into a run, some moving slowly, with great calculation. Jane knew Reb was striding beside her, his face as serious as hers. They heard cries from some of the others behind them but they didn't look back. Long rows of corn stretched ahead. Jane was headed towards them, hoping she would find a kind of sanctuary there. Once she looked back quickly over her shoulder. Grace was behind her, the long fingernails glazed by daybreak. Grace had a triumphant smile on her face. Then Jane saw the boy vulture trotting along briskly, his torso gleaming against the blue sky, his hands trembling in agitation. To her left she saw Miguelito in a grove of dying cherry trees. Farmers were chasing him with a pitchfork and the poor boy was giving little yelps like a dog each time one of the prongs touched his bottom. Jane smiled over at Reb and he returned her smile, wistfully, and shrugged his shoulders. She joined hands with him and they walked on. She hated hearing Miguelito's tormented cries but the faster she walked the more distant and sparse they became and she was soon able to forget them. On and on. The low horizon seemed an endless magnet. And suddenly Jane thought back with a pang of envy as she and her fellow revelers blindly shoved their way through the silent short stalks of harvest corn. Somehow only Cinderella had escaped.

VULTURE

THE RAILS RAN CLOSE TO THE CAROLINA COAST. ON THE ocean side, there were only a few feet of tangled marshes between the tracks and the low waters of the inlet. The inlet was defined by two narrow, rocky promontories, beyond which was the Atlantic, flat and silent in the August heat. On the west side of the tracks were thick woods of oak, cypress, and pine, occasionally broken by a clearing where a run-down house or two stood on the outskirts of town.

It was in these woods that the men paused, waiting for the two o'clock Amtrak to pass by on its way north. The train was late. The men exchanged glances and one of them took a deep breath. Without a word, they set the laundry bag that held Lynn's corpse down on a dry patch. Twigs snapped beneath her weight.

Pat squatted and started scraping mud off his work boots with his pocketknife.

Davy sat on a rock. Pulling the red bandanna off his head, he wiped sweat from his chin, arms, and neck. He fished a pack of Camels from the left sleeve of the T-shirt which gripped his muscular arms. He lit a cigarette. His hands didn't tremble but inside he felt like holy shit. His stomach was like the fucking Atlantic in a storm, all black, wet, and raging. He didn't offer one to Pat, just eased the pack back in his sleeve pocket.

The sunlight found its way to the floor of the woods like sporadic flashlight beams, suddenly pointing here, suddenly there, always changing. *Like it was searching for somebody*, Davy thought. *Like it was searching for two killers*. It was spooky, this dance of light and dark.

Davy forced himself to look at the bag. One of Lynn's hands protruded from the opening. He looked away, up at the sky which was crisscrossed by heavy green leaves on frail branches.

Davy took a drag from his Camel and waited. He didn't wait long. At two-fifteen the train rushed by. Davy couldn't see it, but he felt its hot breeze and heard its rattle. Then it was gone. Pat threw Davy a disgusted look and stood up. Time for business.

The septic tank, corroded and lichen-covered, lay in a clearing between the tracks and the edge of the wood. Together they carried the bag through the brambles into the clearing. Pat lifted the rusty tank lid and looked inside. It was at least twelve feet deep with water at the bottom and its sides were crawling with big red ants, running every which way, startled by the light. By now both of Lynn's bare arms were sticking straight out of the bag. *Rigor mortis*, Davy thought. *Unbendable as logs*.

"Fuck it," Pat read his mind. "Leave her like she is."

They dropped her into the tank. Lynn's arms flailed against the sides as she went down and when the bag hit the bottom there was a small splash.

"Done," said Pat and he wedged the lid back on the tank. But Davy's heart had stopped. About thirty feet away in a patch of swamp grass stood a little girl gazing at the men with curiosity. She was as still and lifeless as a lawn statue and Davy might never have noticed she was there except by chance he'd happened to look in her direction. Now Pat saw her too. His mouth fell open in amazement.

She wore a loose blue cotton dress, much too big for her, that hung from her skinny shoulders like a bedsheet. Her mass of brown curls was uncombed and messy, even though it was tied back from her forehead with a satin blue ribbon. She couldn't have been more than nine or ten. Her gaze was steady. Davy had no idea what she had seen or what she was thinking, but she obviously wasn't afraid. He took a menacing step toward her.

"Hold off, fool," Pat hissed.

The girl took a step backward but she didn't flinch. Her face was expressionless.

"Let's get the hell out of here," Pat said, his voice low and steady.

"But what about her?"

"Forget it, man. Just turn around and walk back into the woods. Slow. Don't act guilty."

But Davy shook his head. "Pat. She saw us."

"Give it up." Pat shoved Davy roughly. "Move."

Davy's brain was exploding inside. But somehow he turned and started walking. Whenever he wavered, he felt Pat's hand on the small of his back, pushing him on. As they reached the cover of the woods, Pat put his arm around Davy's shoulder, all buddy-buddy, but Davy knew they had made a terrible mistake. They had let the girl go when they should have killed her. It was as plain as day. They should have strangled her and dumped her into the tank with Lynn. But they hadn't and now they were in deep shit.

The girl waited until the men had disappeared then cautiously made her way to the clearing. The woods were quiet. There was no sign of the men. To the east, beyond the tracks, she could catch glimpses of the green water of the inlet.

She sat down by the septic tank and put her chin in her hands. The ground was full of life. Beetles weaved in and out of strands of dried moss, a lizard crawled from under a dented Dr. Pepper can, and red ants ran across her sandals.

After awhile the girl decided to lift the lid. It was a struggle at first, but only because it was bulky, not heavy. Once it was off, she leaned over the opening. It took a minute for her eyes to adjust to the blackness. Finally she saw at the bottom two outstretched white arms lifted towards her, almost pleadingly. The girl put a hand over her mouth to stop from crying out. She was looking at death. And in doing so, she understood that the woman with the raised arms could never come back. She sighed, her shoulders sagged, and she took her hand away from her mouth. She pulled the lid back over the opening and stood up. Shaking the ants off her sandals, she turned towards home.

Freeport, South Carolina, lay on the coast twenty miles below the North Carolina border. It was a bleak twenty blocks of bars, groceries, fast-food chains, houses gone to ruin, and long-deserted warehouses, all set ablaze by a wonderland of azaleas, bougainvillea, and lilacs.

These glorious trees and shrubs grew untended and mul-
tiplied with the alarming unpredictability of weeds, jutting
out of broken fence gaps or coloring seedy alleyways. They
were happy accidents.

An orange bougainvillea covered the only window of
Gavin's Grill, a barroom with a wooden counter with eight
stools and two tables along the wall. Inside it was dark at
noon and dark at midnight.

Davy and Pat sat side by side at the counter, smoking and
drinking whiskey. They sat like strangers, afraid to speak,
even afraid to look each other in the eye.

They were determined to get pissed, that was their one
overwhelming need. They had been going at it since leaving
the woods four hours ago. Now it was almost seven-thirty.
The Devil himself couldn't stay sober after drinking shot
after shot like Davy had. Then what was wrong? Why wasn't
he pissed yet? Why did he keep feeling that little girl's eyes
boring into him as he retreated into the woods? What did it
all mean — her calmness and her silence?

Gavin sat by the window, playing solitaire. A couple of
vagrants had wandered in during the afternoon begging for
just one shot, but Gavin had turned them out amid incoher-
ent threats of retaliation and violence. Otherwise the place
had been empty and Davy and Pat had had it to themselves.
But they still couldn't talk because Gavin was all ears. And
they didn't have anything to say yet. They hadn't figured it
all out.

Once, when Gavin went to take a leak, Pat nodded confi-
dently at Davy as if to say, *Lighten up, man, it's fucking A-*

OK. But Davy pouted and carved a deep X into the counter with his pocket knife. They heard the toilet flush and Gavin ambled back in, zipping his fly.

Davy slipped the knife back in his pocket, but drummed on the X with his left index finger. Pat frowned. He didn't get it. He shrugged and took another drink.

Suddenly, Davy slammed the bar with his fist so hard that both Gavin and Pat jumped out of their skins. Davy's pout was gone. It had been replaced by a grim tightening of his lips and clenching of his teeth.

"You two assholes get the hell out of here," Gavin drawled slowly. "Just drop twenty bucks and move on."

"Sorry, man," Pat apologized for Davy, pulling the twenty out of his wallet. "We come up here from Florida about a month ago. My friend here got laid off down in Tallahassee. A bad business. It's hard. Getting used to a new place."

Gavin didn't answer. He didn't even look up. He continued his game of solitaire.

Pat and Davy exchanged glances and Pat motioned for Davy to follow him and they walked out of Gavin's Grill into the musty Freeport sunset. A gull hovered overhead. Three blocks down, half a dozen cars were lining up at the McDonald's drive-thru. Otherwise the town was dead. And that was all right by Davy who for some reason wasn't even pissed.

When Pat told Gavin Davy had been laid off, he wasn't lying. Davy had had a job washing dishes at a Tallahassee pizzeria, but thanks to his being high every day on alcohol and marijuana, he was undependable and careless, arriving late for his shift and dropping glasses with such regularity that his boss, glued to the cash register but with an ear to the kitchen, could begin to predict when each "accident" would occur. One every fifteen minutes.

He took Davy aside. "Hey, look, bud, this isn't a shooting gallery. Each time you drop a glass, you're costing me money."

Davy had started to chuckle uncontrollably. His boss paid him a week's wages and fired him.

"Down but not out," Davy had mumbled to his girlfriend, Lynn Smith, and to reward himself for surviving the unpleasant experience of being canned, he had driven the dilapidated van his brother had sold him to a tattoo parlor on the south side and had had his left arm decorated with a beautiful red rose.

Lynn had seemed pleased as hell. She was a scrawny little blonde who spent her energies shuffling from one man to another, trying to find one that would keep her for a while and let her catch her breath. Davy Collins was a vain twenty-four-year-old, well-built, with thick blond bangs framing an almost cherubic face that he had hardened by growing a thick yellow mustache and sideburns. Lynn was savvy enough to see that she could score points by praising his good looks, and when he showed off his new tattoo she rose to the occasion and ran her tongue over the crimson petals, gazing all the while into his eyes as if he were God. He had blushed and given a sheepish grin, then had kissed her tenderly on the lips.

It was about this time that Davy's buddy, Pat Fowler, had

decided that the three of them were going nowhere. Pat was thirty, dark, short, and wiry and had been around, doing odd construction jobs and, during layoffs, dealing drugs. But he was tired of dealing and wanted a permanent job. He convinced Davy and Lynn to kiss Tallahassee good-bye and set off with him for the New York – New Jersey area where construction jobs were rumored to be plentiful and secure. They had piled into Davy's van and headed north, but by the time they reached Freeport they had run out of money. They decided to spend the last of their funds to rent an apartment and see if Lynn couldn't get a minimum wage job to support everybody, just temporarily, while the men nosed around for construction work.

But Lynn never had a chance to go job-hunting, since she was killed a week after setting up house in Freeport.

"Don't you want to know about the X?" Davy asked as they smoked some weed and stared without interest at the mildewed Monopoly board on the kitchen table.

"I figure you'll let me know when you're ready," Pat answered, piqued. "I'm not gonna twist your arm."

"What's with you, man?" Davy asked. "That girl. She saw us hide Lynn in the tank."

"She's a little girl. She probably sees killer whales playing every day in the Atlantic or fairies under toadstools. Little girls have great imaginations."

"Bullshit. She didn't imagine what she saw today. And one word from her and we're cooked."

The three-room apartment was hot, blinds drawn against

the last sun rays. No fan to move the air. Pat got an ice cube from the freezer and ran it across his forehead. He shook his finger at Davy and said slowly, "All this is your fault. You got bad blood in your veins."

"You're in this up to your ears, you asshole, and you know it."

Pat shrugged and moved into the living room where he spread out on the sofa, the only piece of furniture in the room. Water marks on the ceiling became pulsating galaxies fixed in eternity. The weed and whiskey had done their job. He closed his eyes.

In the kitchen, Davy flipped through the Monopoly money. If only he could spend this multicolored paper, he'd be in California in the blink of an eye.

Lynn had sat there flipping the same money the night she died. She had been perched on a kitchen stool, scrutinizing the phony hundreds of thousands and the property cards when he'd confronted her. Had she been thinking along the same lines as he was now? She always claimed she wanted to end up in Hawaii. Had she been dreaming of a new life there, close to the surf and the sand? Probably not. No doubt she'd been wondering how to ditch him and take off with Pat.

"Fuck you," Davy shouted in to Pat. "You know what we have to do to stay alive."

"What?" Pat's voice trailed back to him, disembodied, mellow. "What do we have to do?"

"That X I carved. It meant we have to kill that girl. We have to stop her from being able to identify us."

"You're loony," came the response.

And then they both passed out. The oblivion they had

tried to summon up had finally come in a quick rush of heat and exhaustion.

The next morning Davy slipped out of the apartment while Pat was still sleeping it off, climbed into the van and drove aimlessly through town until he came upon Freeport's only elementary school. The building itself was unremarkable, a low concrete square with a fenced playground off to one side, but like many other edifices in town, it benefited from a virtual jungle of red bougainvillea, spiraling off its roof like fireworks and giving the school a fantastic air. The playground bordered a quiet street and Davy parked close to the fence.

His intent was to identify the girl when she came out to play at recess. He definitely didn't want to be seen by any busybodies as he sat there waiting for her, but that was unlikely. On the other side of the street was a sloping green hill on which lilac bushes rustled in the wind, reluctant to give up any of their silver-lavender blooms. Lopsided tombstones were set among the bushes and Davy realized he was looking at an unfenced, untended cemetery, the bodies laid to rest haphazardly, one tombstone only inches away from the curb.

He looked away and lit a Camel. The gusts of wind blew the smoke into his eyes and he remembered his dream. Lynn had been alive and they had walked together through a burning, smoke-filled landscape, giggling foolishly, relieved to be safe in such a catastrophic place. As flames tore at their heels, Lynn had kept repeating, "I'm alive, I'm alive, I'm alive." Then a flame had lapped at his left arm and the rose began to melt, the petals formless and ugly, like a glob of sugar candy cooking in the sun. Finally the tattoo evaporated completely. Unlike the smoke and the flames and the hovering figure of Lynn, his white, bare arm gave him a fright.

A bell sounded sharply and recess was called. Davy checked his watch: ten AM. He slumped a little in his seat and pulled the red bandanna over his forehead, covering his hair. Out of the corner of his eye he saw the boys and girls rush out into the playground. Some headed for the swings, others began tossing a volleyball, while others formed little cliques off to the side, whispering secrets together. Was she one of the ones whispering, and if so, what secrets was she revealing?

He began to sweat, not just his face but his whole body. He was as wet as a sponge. He silently smoked another Camel, staring straight ahead, trying to appear inconspicuous and disinterested in what was happening in the playground. But he wasn't doing a good job. He was fidgeting in his seat and when he caught a glimpse of his eyes in the rearview mirror, he saw they were as big as silver dollars.

It wasn't until he heard the bell go off again, signifying an end to recess, that he summoned up enough courage to look into the playground. And this time, right away, he saw her. As the other children began to file grudgingly into the building, she sat alone, quietly, as still as he'd seen her yesterday. She was hunched against the wall, her back against the cascading strands of red bougainvillea. Today she wore a white cotton dress, but her tangled hair was swept back with the same blue satin ribbon. There was no mistaking her. She was staring at him with mild interest, as she might at an animal in a zoo, an animal she was already familiar with. How long had she been watching him? He didn't know.

With a quick, bold movement, he gestured for her to come over to the van. Still gazing at him, she got to her feet and carefully smoothed her white cotton dress, then followed the last of the children back into school.

What Pat didn't know was that, while Lynn's corpse had lain on the kitchen floor and he'd sat slumped at the kitchen table deciding what to do, Davy was busy rummaging through Lynn's purse in the bedroom. Davy figured he'd find a little cash but he ended up striking pay dirt. He discovered seven hundred dollars in a zippered compartment. He put it in his wallet, then dropped three dollars in loose change in the purse, so that when, an hour later, he emptied the contents on the bed in front of Pat, they went diving for only a few quarters and dimes scattered among cheap cosmetics, keys, and bric-a-brac souvenirs Lynn had picked up on the trip north.

Davy wasn't eager to part with Lynn's money, but his plans called for him to while away a few hours and return to the school around two o'clock so he could follow the girl home and find out where she lived. He didn't want to go back to the apartment and get into a hassle with Pat. So he bought a fishing rod and some tackle in a sporting goods store, then drove to the inlet not far from the tank where Lynn's body was hidden.

He walked out onto the stone-covered promontory which seemed to be a popular fishing spot, since about half a dozen other men stood at lonely intervals, like sentinels, casting their lines out to sea. Though there was nothing of a sentinel's bearing or purpose about any of them, only a bored indolence.

As it turned out, Davy was less inclined to fish than to sleep, as he was still suffering from a hangover. He chose a pine whose shade was generous and stretched out beneath the refuge of needles.

Before him the water of the inlet moved about churlishly under a strong sun.

There were a few clouds overhead whose edges were a ghostly emerald green, as if they reflected the essence of the sea.

Suddenly Davy felt a stirring inside him. He wanted to make love to a woman, but Lynn had been the only woman he'd been sleeping with. He didn't know any others. Well, he'd screwed things up all right. He was alone.

When Davy woke up it was just past three o'clock. Surely school had already let out and he'd missed his chance to follow the girl home. Or had he? Maybe she was leaving now, lingering behind in her slow way to pick some of the flowers of the bougainvillea.

He raced to his van and gunned it at about 70 m.p.h. up to the railway tracks. He jerked to a halt at the crossing as the warning lights were flashing and he knew the two o'clock Amtrak train was late again, as late as he was, and ready to round the bend.

He waited impatiently, tempted to run the light, figuring once he crossed over, he'd be near town and forced to observe the speed limit to avoid being pulled over by a cop. Out of the corner of his eye he saw the silver flash of the train approaching, while directly in front of him, across the tracks, he saw a tiny figure in a white cotton dress coming down the road. Then the train sped by, blocking his view, and he wondered if, in fear, he'd conjured up the sweet, silent figure he desperately wanted to find. But when the train had passed, and his view was clear, he saw that it was her, turning now onto a side road that ran parallel to the tracks, apparently unaware that he was watching her.

Davy backed his van up and parked it a few feet away in a sandy enclave protected by a circle of stunted oak trees. Then he took off on foot along the tracks in the direction the girl had gone.

It wasn't long until he came to the clearing where a wooden cottage, painted blue, rose out of the low swamplands. Its screened-in porch had a picture perfect view of the rails and, consequently, of him. He crouched low and watched the girl go into the house via the porch.

So here was where she lived, in a virtual wilderness, and she walked by herself back and forth to school. To intercept her along the way would be child's play.

He understood how she had chanced upon them as they were disposing of Lynn's body; she had simply been out for a solitary walk not far from her home.

Suddenly the screen door banged open and the girl flew out of the house, pursued by an angry woman with a broom held threateningly in her right hand. The girl was running fast, right towards him, and he cursed, crouching lower, flattening his nose to the rails. The woman froze midway in the yard, unwilling to give chase, and, dropping the broom, she called in a pitiful voice for the girl to come back. The girl stopped before she reached the tracks. Davy felt sure she hadn't seen him. She wheeled around and the woman held both arms out to her. The girl eagerly returned to her, with a kind of light dancing gait, and they held each other close, rocking back and forth.

Even though strands of baby-fine blonde hair hung down into the woman's face, obscuring her features, Davy could tell from her bearing and behavior that she was the girl's mother.

After awhile she gave a last caress to her daughter and went back inside.

The girl picked her way gingerly through the swamp grass to the train tracks, until she was only a dozen or so feet from where he lay prostrate, holding his breath. His eyes watched her as she gazed into the distance toward the Atlantic. It seemed an eternity before she had her fill of the scenery and decided to return to the house.

When Davy got up, he noticed a set of wind chimes hanging from the low branch of a cypress at the far end of the clearing. As he crept along the tracks toward his van a breeze came up and he heard the chimes jangling.

That night Davy and Pat dined at McDonald's on fish sandwiches and french fries. Then they dared to return to Gavin's for a round of drinks. The bar was crowded so they settled down at a table against the wall. Gavin served them whiskey with no reference to their past unpleasant parting. Davy guessed he would all right. Their money was as green as anybody else's. But they couldn't help noticing that Gavin smirked as he set their glasses in front of them.

"He'll get his in the end," Davy muttered. "His type always does. They look the wrong way at the wrong guy and it's good-bye Señor Gavin."

"Are you always thinking of revenge? Always thinking of getting somebody? A shrink would have a field day with you, buddy."

"They already have. When I did time in a Miami detention center when I was fifteen. All I did was steal a beat-up Chrysler and you'd think I'd planned to gun down the president for all the cockeyed questions they asked me." Davy lit a Camel. "Anyway, good friend, a shrink might like to ask you a few particulars. Like how come you don't give a shit if a kid gets hooked on the dope you deal."

Pat ignored him. He whispered, "One death isn't enough for you. You killed Lynn. Wasn't that enough? Do you have to babble on about killing a little girl? Or that you hope Gavin gets his? . . . Well, do you?"

Davy knew Pat's game. He hadn't mentioned anything about the girl since last night. This was Pat's way of pumping him for information. Pat wanted the girl dead, too, only he didn't want to admit it. He wanted Davy to take care of it all by himself so he wouldn't get his hands bloodied.

"What about that X you carved on the bar over there? What kind of jerk would do that? What was that supposed to mean?"

"Nothing."

"Nothing?" Pat hissed quietly. "Last night you told me it meant something. Didn't you?"

Davy took a drag from his cigarette and changed the subject to the weather, just to get at Pat. But Pat cut him off. He asked Davy what he'd done all day. Davy lied that he'd hoofed it along the business loop in search of construction work. Nothing doing.

They fell silent and continued to drink.

Once Pat, in a carefully planned absent-minded moment, traced an X in front of Davy with his right forefinger.

Davy yawned and said it was late. They'd better get home.

The next afternoon at two o'clock Davy parked his van once again in the oak-shrouded enclave on the rocky promontory, then jumped the tracks and headed up the road to the wooded intersection that was the girl's turnoff.

Clouds hung low in the sky, but it didn't feel like rain. But it was still hot and his T-shirt clung to him like a wet rag.

Animals rustled noisily in the woods and made their presence known but no cars passed him.

She came down the road at three. He'd waited almost an hour behind some moss a little way along the mud-encrusted road that led to her cottage. In fact he could see its black tile roof from where he stood.

She was wearing blue jeans and a peach-colored blouse and the ever-present blue satin ribbon in her hair. As she neared his hiding place, he stepped forward directly into her path. She showed a little surprise, but nothing more.

"Hey," he said.

She didn't answer.

"What's that sound? Chimes. There must be wind chimes somewhere around. You must know about them." He couldn't hear them from this distance, of course he couldn't, but there was a little wind blowing leaves down the road and it was the only thing he could think of to engage her in conversation. "They sound real pretty," he continued in a rush. "I like that sound. You know about them I bet. Maybe you'd like to take me through the woods and show me where they are."

"Who are you?" she asked evenly.

"Never mind that." Then when she didn't respond he asked, "What's your name?"

"Peggy."

"Maybe you'll show me where the wind chimes are. You've hidden them I bet. Let's make a game of it. Why don't you take me through the woods and see if I'm smart enough to find them? Would you like that, Peggy?"

"What do you really want?" she asked. "Why did you come to my school?"

"Your school?" he stammered. "I never went to your school. You saw somebody else."

She persisted. "What do you want?"

He felt like yelling that he wanted her to lead him into the woods so he could strangle her with his red bandanna. It would only take a minute for him to rip it off his head and wrap it around her throat.

"Peggy," he calmly said instead, "I want to be your friend."

He blushed with the lie.

"Why?"

"I don't have many friends."

"I have to go now."

"Peggy . . . can I ask you something? Let's say you did see me at your school. But did you ever see me before that?"

"Of course. You and that other man. By the tank a few days ago."

He shivered. "With another man? A few days ago? By a tank? Not me."

"It was you." She tossed her hair back with an almost imperious air.

"Why do you say that?"

"The rose on your arm. I remember it."

Guiltily, he clutched at his tattooed arm with his right hand in an effort to hide the rose from her. But it was too big to cover. And when he saw her studying it wistfully, he slowly let his hand fall away.

"So you see," she said softly. "It was you. I know by the rose."

He peered at her closely. "What else did you see that day?"

"I saw her. I looked down inside and saw her arms."

"I see."

The wind picked up a little and her thick hair blew around her face.

"Did you tell?"

She looked at him wonderingly.

"Don't play the innocent with me," he snapped. "Who did

you tell about it?"

"Nobody."

Davy's mind reeled. She had been truthful about every-thing else. Maybe she was telling the truth now.

"But it was bad," she added. "Very wicked. To put some-body down there."

"But you didn't tell?"

"You're afraid." It was a simple statement, uttered quietly, but Davy felt the weight of her words. And they were very heavy.

"No," he repled unconvincingly.

"I have to go home now."

"What if I didn't let you go home? What if I told you you were never going home again?" Furious, he shook his finger in her face. "What if I put you down in that tank with . . . with her?"

Frightened, she stumbled back a few steps and shook her head.

In a flash he saw that he needed to buy time. He couldn't kill her here, along this road. It was all wrong. He needed time to think.

He fell to his knees. "Come here . . . please."

She frowned and her lips quivered slightly.

"Come here. I would never do it. I couldn't." He held out his arms to her. Again she eyed the rose. "Just give me a chance. Meet me one more time. Just to talk to me. I don't want to hurt you. Just one more time. Tomorrow. I'll come back here and wait for you."

Slowly she approached him and he flung his arms around

her legs and looked up into her face. "Only promise me. Promise you won't say anything about me or the tank until I talk to you again tomorrow. You're a good girl, an honest girl. Just promise me and I'll believe you."

Her mouth opened but no words came out.

"Promise me," he begged. "Promise . . ."

"I promise." Then she moved around him and went home leaving him on his knees.

That night he relived Lynn's last hour.

He lay on the bed listening to Pat splashing around in the bathtub. The smell of marijuana drifted in to him and it got Davy's goat that Pat could get high and enjoy a good soak, even though he was responsible for everything.

If only he could have that hour back, could rearrange it like an errant daydream gone sour, mold it to his liking. But wasn't life just one big "if only"? If only I hadn't been born. If only I didn't have to die. If only I could live my life as a blonde. Reinventing was the secret of the life force, of all human energy.

He had never suspected Lynn and Pat. Her dogged devotion to him suggested that somewhere along the line he'd be the one to have to break the relationship off, letting her down as gently as possible.

That night it had been his turn to go out for food. He picked up a bucket of chicken and slaw at the Kentucky Fried drive-thru. There was no line. He got back fast. Fast enough to interrupt Lynn and Pat during a quickie in the kitchen. Lynn was bent over the stove and Pat was standing behind her. There was an awkward flurry of pants being pulled up and throats being cleared.

No one said a word. Davy dropped the food on the kitchen table and Lynn scurried around for plates. Pat took three beers out of the refrigerator.

After dinner Lynn brought out a Monopoly game she'd found in the bedroom closet. The box was damp, mold had eaten away at the corners of the board, but all the pieces were there. She set it up at the kitchen table and, settling down on a stool, started leafing through the money. Davy leaned against the stove, arms crossed, watching her.

"This should be something different," Pat muttered as he headed for the bathroom to take a leak.

"Why?" Davy asked her. "Why did you do it?"

"Pat wanted it. It was nothing against you. I still love you. But Pat has been the odd man out. He was lonely. He needed a little affection."

"And you obliged him like a cheap tramp."

Lynn bristled. "It was the first time we did it. And it'll be the last. You'll have to understand."

He was incredulous. "You think I want to sleep with you now? Well, I don't." His face turned red. "The two of you can have all the fun you want."

"Fine, then," Lynn replied, hurt. "If you don't want me, he does. It wasn't so bad with him anyway."

"You lewd bitch!" Davy cried and sprang at her. He yanked her off the stool by her hair and, in a rage, slammed her face down on top of the stove. He heard something crack and thought it was one of the gas rings, but when he saw the split in her head and the blood pouring down her face he realized he'd shattered her skull. Shocked, he let go of her hair and she slumped onto the kitchen floor.

Pat appeared in the doorway. His face registered little emotion. He knelt down by Lynn and cradled her head in his lap. Davy looked on. Pat finally checked for her pulse. There wasn't any.

"Jesus Christ," Pat said. "I go in to take a piss, am gone less than a minute, and when I come back in here I find my whole fucking life has changed."

Davy laughed uneasily. He couldn't help it. But throughout the night he cried. He was frightened and ashamed.

Pat kept his cool. The next morning he left Davy alone to scour the woods for a possible hiding place for Lynn's body. That's when he'd come upon the perfect burial ground, the septic tank.

Davy's initial anger towards Pat dissipated as soon as Lynn was dead. Pat was his buddy, after all. And he was helping him out in his hour of need. What would he have done if it had been just him alone, with Lynn lying there? He'd have cracked up and called it a day. He didn't want to be by himself. He wanted Pat's company. They were in it together.

Or were they? As Davy listened to Pat letting the water out of the tub he realized that a distance had come between them, a lack of trust. There was the usual small talk and drinking and smoking together. But there was no communication, a blind was drawn against the future.

For instance, Davy couldn't bring himself to tell Pat about his encounter with Peggy. Pat would have told him off, all the while insinuating in his subtle way that Davy should go ahead and get it over with. Davy didn't like Pat's furtiveness, his dishonesty. When Davy killed Peggy, he wouldn't even tell Pat. The two of them would be safe, but Pat wouldn't know it. Let him sweat it out a little.

Yet thinking it over carefully, Davy figured Pat would find out about it. The whole town would, the whole state. Maybe the whole country would read the story of a little girl's strangled body found in the South Carolina woods. Peggy's death would have to be an accident. It was too messy, too dangerous any other way.

Pat came into the room, toweling himself dry.

"What are you thinking about," he asked, "lying there like a robot?"

"Robots don't think," Davy said.

"No, they act."

"Not always," Davy answered. "There must be a million stories in Robotland."

"Yeah, sure, a million."

"Got some weed for me?"

"I'm running low, man. I won't always have nice things for you. Especially when you never pay me nothin'."

"When my ship comes in, Pat, I'll pay you back in spades."

Pat threw the towel in Davy's face and insulted him. "Lousy lowlife."

"Just bring me some weed. And a beer . . ."

"Get off your ass and get it yourself. The weed's in the kitchen drawer . . ." He paused. "The one next to the stove."

Davy didn't honor Pat with a reaction.

Pat continued, "And there's beer in the refrigerator. I'm gonna crash on the sofa. And don't wake me up. I don't want to see your face. It gives me bad dreams."

"Thanks, good buddy, for your encouraging words."

"Look man, it's your fault I'm in this mess and not up in New York with a good job and a clear conscience. We could be arrested any time now when that girl decides to talk. There could be a knock at the door any day. Any night. And when it comes, you could be sitting on the john, fixing breakfast, looking out the window at the birds, and that'll be the last thing you ever do as a free man."

She was as good as her word. She went through with the meeting. Even though she'd gotten home earlier than usual and passed the mossy hiding place before he'd even parked his van. It was just as he arrived at their prearranged spot that he saw her coming down the road from the direction of her house. Quickly he pulled the sleeves of his T-shirt over his shoulder to make sure his tattoo was exposed, but she didn't give it a second glance today.

"I don't want to see you anymore," she said emphatically. "What you did was very wrong."

He smiled a little. "You came here just to tell me that?"

"Yes."

He changed the subject. "School get out early today?"

"No. I just walked faster. I wanted to get home before you got here."

"Oh, yeah?"

"I wasn't going to meet you here. Only . . ."

"Only what?"

"I promised."

"That's right. You have to keep your promises to friends."

"You're not my friend."

Davy took a deep breath. "I'd like to change your mind about that. I want you to let me explain everything. I want you to give me a chance to tell you what happened and why it happened. So that if you decide to tell somebody about me, about the tank, you'll know the whole story."

He could tell she was giving his words some thought and wanted to hear more.

"I don't want to hurt you," he continued. "God knows I don't. If I wanted to I could drag you into the woods right now. But I don't want to."

In her face he sensed a loneliness he hadn't noticed before, an eagerness to believe him. Why wouldn't she be lonely, living in the backwoods with her mother? He hadn't seen her with any friends, either on that fateful walk when she first saw him or in the playground at school.

"I deserve a chance to clear myself, don't I?"

"Well? Go ahead."

"Not here. You live in the house in the clearing, don't you? The one just down the road? I've seen it."

It didn't seem to surprise her that he knew where she lived. But as if she suspected he was ready to invite himself over she blurted, "You can't come in."

"Of course not," he answered impatiently. "I know that. But we could go somewhere else. Meet up a little later. Say about seven. We could walk across to the inlet. Sit down and

have a long talk. I could tell you about what happened . . .
between her and me . . . every secret . . ."

"Every secret . . ." she murmured.

"That's right. Then we can be friends," he said. "Once you
know everything."

The sun beat down on them.

Above the pines, the sky was a rich, clear gold, completely
free of clouds.

"I'll wait for you by the tracks behind your house," Davy
said soothingly.

"Yes," she said.

This time it was Davy who walked away, with a carefree
air, hoping to give the impression that he had no harmful
intentions toward her. As he turned onto the main road he
saw that she was still rooted there, watching him. Cheerfully,
he waved. She didn't wave back.

He spent the remainder of the afternoon wandering
around the promontory, combing the rocky shore for a
promising killing spot, one that was sheltered from view. At
the hour of their rendezvous it was likely they would be
alone. But there was no guarantee. There were no fishermen
out now, but that didn't preclude the possibility that one
might come along at dusk. Davy didn't want to take any
chances.

He studied the protected expanse of water that was
attached to the Atlantic and wondered why he hadn't thought
of drowning her before. That was the safest route of all.

If her body were discovered washed ashore, her death
would be seen as an accident. She had strayed from home

and slipped off the rocks and drowned. An unforeseen tragedy, nothing more. Maybe her body would drift to Spain or be pulled in a tangle of weeds to the bottom of the sea. That would be even better.

Halfway down the promontory there was a break in the rocks. Water flowed inland to form several deep pools. Though the area was exposed, not really to his liking, the dark should afford all the protection he'd need. He'd hold her head under water, and when she was dead carry her body to the inlet and cast her adrift.

At seven he was waiting by the tracks. The sun was still warm and bathed the yard in a somber bronze light. But in the shady recesses of the woods, where the trees grew thick and close, lightning bugs were already blinking in starlike patterns.

Closing the screen door gently, she approached him tentatively, dressed in the ill-fitting blue cotton dress she'd worn that first day. Gone was the blue satin ribbon, her hair held back with barrettes. He gave her a comforting pat on the shoulder and they quickly made their way onto the promontory, which glittered from the sun-splashed reflection of the water. The rocks seemed to be finely polished and the thin layers of sand wedged between them were as clean and soft as sugar. In the Atlantic a steamer made quick passage south. Peggy removed her sandals and walked barefoot.

They settled down on a flat grey rock that slanted down towards the inlet.

"It'll be fun to watch the stars come out over the water,"

Davy remarked.

"I see them all the time from my window," she said in a bored tone.

"It'll be fun to watch them just the same. I can't see them from where I live."

"Where's that?"

"In town. I have a couple of rooms. Nothing special. I live by myself. It can get pretty lonesome."

"It gets lonesome out here too. But I have the trains going by. I can hear them coming a long way off. And I get excited and always go to the window no matter what time it is and watch them pass by."

"Ever been on one of them?"

"No. I don't want to either. I just like to watch. They go so fast and jerk from side to side. I can just imagine all the people falling, dropping their coffee cups, getting sick."

He laughed. "It's not that way at all. They don't feel much. They're just glad to get where they're going."

"I don't want to go anywhere."

"No? Well, neither do I. I thought I did once. Thought I wanted to go to New York. But I'm kind of settled here now. I'm pretty happy where I am . . ." He gave her a hard stare. "You're a funny kid. You mean to tell me even if it's three in the morning you get out of bed to see an old Amtrak go by?"

"Every night."

He shrugged. "Who do you live with? Your mom and dad?"

"Just my mom."

"No brothers? Sisters?"

"Don't have any."

"Your dad. Where's he at?"

"One night a hurricane came along the coast. Mom and me went down to the cellar, scared out of our wits. But he came out here, way out to land's end . . ." She pointed all the way down the promontory. "He wanted to see the big waves but Mom says he got too careless and waited in a dangerous spot and one of them swallowed him up."

Fat chance, Davy thought. There hadn't been any hurricane fatalities of that type for years. He'd have heard about a bimbo who went to frolic in the coming storm and came to a bad end. That kind of story always makes the front pages. More than likely he slipped out of town during the storm and Peggy's mom lied about it.

To make sure he asked, "Where did they find his body?"

She turned to him, tears in her eyes, and said, "They never did. They never found him."

Davy wanted to tell her to cut the crap. He wasn't in the mood for a sob story. But he wanted to stay on her good side and said, "Tough luck."

Her face was red and puffy. She brushed away a tear and smiled at him warmly as if his were the kindest words she'd ever heard. Horrified, he realized he was a father figure to her. He cleared his throat.

"Well," he said. "We didn't come here to talk about your dad. It makes you too sad. Here," he offered his bandanna. "Dry your eyes."

She gave her eyes a few dabs then handed it back to him.

"That's better," he said. "Now I want to tell you about what happened. That woman that you saw in the tank. Her name was Lynn and she was very wicked. She lived on a big farm not far from here with her father who was dying of cancer. Times had been rough for a few years and her old man was in danger of losing the place. But he couldn't work the land himself and hoped that she would help him. He gave her his last savings and sent her into Freeport to hire a few able-bodied men. She went into town all right but she spent the money drinking and drugging and buying pretty baubles she didn't need. When she'd spent all the money, she picked up men who paid her to sleep with them. They paid her well for her filthy work. But she didn't send any money home, she kept it all for herself. Well, one day she found she was pregnant. She did go home then to have the baby. It was a beautiful baby boy. With fine blond hair and blue eyes. Hey. You know who he looked like?"

"No," she said. "Who?"

"Me. I was the father. She had come to me one night and told me how lonely she was. I fell for her. Lynn phoned me and told me I was the father. But she didn't want me to see the baby. She was planning to sell it for a thousand dollars and move to Hawaii. Well, I couldn't let that happen. I told her I was coming out to the farm to claim the boy as I was his father and wanted to raise him. She laughed and hung up on me. I drove out there as fast as I could, even though it was midnight and a storm had come up and I could barely see the road. When I got there I was soaked to the bone. Exhausted. I pounded on the door, but she wouldn't let me in. I had to break a pane of glass in the kitchen window and crawl inside. She was sitting on a stool by the kitchen table, a picture of innocence. And do you know what she was doing?"

Peggy shook her head.

"She had a Monopoly board spread out on the table and she was flipping through the stacks of paper money, greedily counting it, as if it was the real stuff. My heart sank since I could see she'd lost her mind. I ran through the house until I came to a bedroom at the end of the hall. I opened the door and my whole life changed in just a minute. Her father was in bed, my baby boy lying in his arms. But they were dead. She'd poisoned them both." He let out a sob. "I was overcome with rage. I dashed back to the kitchen and confronted her. She was glad to see me so broken, so torn up inside. I yanked her up by the hair and she fell against the stove. She hit her head and died. I didn't kill her. It was an accident. But who'd believe me? It was like she died on purpose, willed it to happen, to spite me. But she deserved it. Someone that wicked can't continue to make her way in the world.

"I gave her father and my son a decent burial on the farm.

"And you know the rest. I hid her body in the tank where she'd never be found."

"But who was that man with you?"

He blinked but came up with a fast response. "Her brother. He hated her as much as I did."

Peggy's expression was one of sadness, of regret. He could tell she felt for him.

"So you believe me?"

"Yes, I do."

For a brief moment he was overcome with relief. She had bought it. And maybe her pity would assure her silence.

There might not be a need for him to silence her after all.

His bubble burst a moment later when she said, "But it's wrong to leave Lynn down there. As bad as she was, she deserves to be buried like anyone else."

He was stunned by her final words — "So you can visit her and bring flowers to a real grave."

"That's ridiculous!" he exploded. "You want someone so low to have a proper grave covered with flowers?"

"It's only right."

"That means you're going to tell?"

"I don't know. Maybe. I don't know. I can't bear to think of her lying in the dark all alone."

"She's dead, for Christ's sake!"

"I can't bear it. It's a terrible secret," she cried miserably.

So. That was how the land lay. He'd have to kill her and be done with it, just as he'd planned. He was safe now, but she was wavering, suffering from an odd guilt that had nothing to do with her. She wanted to blurt it all out. Then where would he be?

The pools were waiting for her, as surely as the night was deepening, fast on the sinking of the bloated, gold sun.

"I'm going to take you to see something fascinating. To a pool where silver fishes glow in the dark."

"Really?" She perked up, shedding that hangdog look she'd had since the sun set. "Where?"

"Down aways."

"My dad never mentioned seeing any. And he was out here a lot."

"He didn't know everything, did he? I fish along here at night. And I'm telling you what I saw."

He led her towards the pools. The air was clear for an August night and crisp and the stars flickered white and blue from their faraway placements in the heavens. The tips of the pines were set aglow by the light of a new moon. As they walked along, they stepped on the sharply-etched silhouettes of rocks. There was no one else around.

There wasn't any need for magical silver fishes, the night had its own spell. But Peggy seemed intrigued by the thought of them. She grabbed his hand, but he roughly pulled it away.

"They're something else," Davy said with bravado. "They dart around like wildfire under the water. They must come in with the tide. Strange creatures all lit up."

He stopped cold. The pools lay in their path down a slight sandy decline.

"Come on, let's take a look."

He knelt by the largest pool and motioned for her to join him.

She lay her sandals down on the sand and slipped to her knees.

They were side by side, peering into the pool.

"You have to look real close. Bend your head down."

She lowered her face a little and stared into the pool.

"See anything?" he asked.

She was silent. It was obvious that there were no silver fishes. She saw only the dark, ominous surface of the pool.

Without looking up she asked softly, "Should I pray now?"

With a cry he jumped up and stumbled backwards, falling

on the decline. "Don't say that!"

She didn't turn around but continued to stare into the pool's depths.

He gained his equilibrium and started running down the promontory. The stars, the sky, the trees seemed to shake as he ran, shake and break apart.

Davy had no memory of his drive home except for the vague feeling that he had recklessly run some lights, but he was all in one piece, sprawled out on his bed.

It was past midnight and Pat was still out. That was odd. But Davy was grateful for some breathing room so he could gain some composure, for what it was worth.

As he lay there, alone, he saw himself for what he was. A man who was impulsive, who had never meant to kill Lynn, but who had been driven to strike out at her in a hot blinding rage.

Killing Peggy was something else. Premeditated. Disgraceful. He couldn't go through with it, even if it meant that her words could lead to his arrest. He figured it would be either a hard-hearted or thick-skulled jury that would convict a man for lashing out at his girlfriend when he'd just caught her humping his buddy when his back was turned. Or if they did convict him it would be for manslaughter. He wouldn't have to do much time. How much? If fate was cruel . . . let's see . . . and he got, say, three years . . . he'd probably only have to serve around six months. Get sprung early for good behavior. And he'd be an angel all right.

He counted six on his fingers. Six months. He could get

through it. Would it be worth drowning Peggy over that short a stay in prison? And if he did kill her and somehow got caught, well, they'd lock his ass up till it rotted.

It wasn't in his interest to kill her, and God knows it wasn't in hers.

He'd bite the bullet. It wouldn't be the first time.

He thought of her kneeling there, gazing into that dark circle of water, so sinister because it was to be her pool of death. Now, with immense relief, he thought of Peggy ambling home and the pool unrippled, the surface unbroken, just like the night before and the night to come. Nothing had happened. Nothing would have to.

Mornings are supposed to bring a balm to troubled souls, the streaks of dawn diluting the paranoid introspection that grows tumorlike in the black small hours, but it didn't work that way. Davy had had an undisturbed rest, brought about no doubt by his new resolve. But the minute he woke up to the sounds of birds and the coral glow that softened every corner, he felt uneasy. He sensed an emptiness in the next room.

He lay in bed, not eager to get up. Again he counted six on his fingers. Then again and again until it meant nothing to him. Eventually he screwed up enough courage to go into the living room. The sofa hadn't been slept on. He opened the closet door and Pat's clothes and suitcase were missing.

The bastard had run out on him. Probably taken the train to New York. No note. No good-bye. He'd screwed Lynn, helped dispose of her body, then, when the heat was on and he'd realized Davy wasn't going to kill the girl, he'd split. Well, fine.

Last night as he had drifted off, Davy had decided he'd make some morning rounds at a couple of offices downtown to see if he could drum up some construction work. He'd take anything. Lynn's money wouldn't last forever. But now he felt down, the victim of a low trick, Pat leaving him in limbo.

He drove out to the inlet instead to do some fishing. He stayed there all day, baking in the sun, and catching only two fishes so small they'd fit nicely together in a goldfish bowl.

That night he went into Gavin's Grill and got loaded.

"Where's your pal?" Gavin asked in an insolent tone, his face deadpan.

"He died of an overdose," Davy answered. "Want the address of the funeral parlor so you can send flowers?"

"I got better things to do with my money."

During the next few days Davy hardly left his apartment. He went out to pick up dinner at McDonald's but that was it. He was depressed and couldn't shake it.

One morning he just got up, didn't bother to dress, went directly to the refrigerator, pulled out a six-pack of Miller, planted himself on the sofa, drank one after the other while chain-smoking a pack of Camels.

That's the morning the knock on the door came. At first he thought it was Pat, come back from God knows where. But Pat had his own set of keys.

The knock came again. Suddenly Davy realized it was *the* knock, the one Pat had told him about. Only he wasn't doing any of the things Pat had described. He wasn't sitting on the john, fixing breakfast, or looking out the window at the birds. He was sitting in his underpants in a cloud of stale smoke, beer stains on the floor, just staring straight at the door. Like some animal. They'd see he was no good and hold it against him. He wouldn't answer. They could break the door down if they wanted him that bad. But the knock wasn't repeated and he heard footsteps shuffling away.

The knock came again after midnight. He was in bed, asleep. He woke up with a start, terrified. He felt like pulling the covers over his head and disappearing forever.

Then a voice called out, "Come on, Pat, open the door, I know you're in there, goddamit."

Pat? Who the hell wanted him? Puzzled, Davy walked to the door.

"Who is it?" His voice was barely above a whisper.

"Pat?"

"No. He's not here."

"I'm tired of this bullshit. Open the door, man."

Davy opened the door a crack. A bearded young man with a silver earring glowered at him.

When Davy saw it wasn't the cops, his confidence returned in spades.

"Why the fuck are you waking me up at twelve-thirty in the morning?"

The man's voice was gruff but tentative. "I want to see Pat."

"Why?"

"He owes me some weed, that's why. I gave him a fifty buck deposit five days ago. I brought the other fifty and now

I want the shit."

"Pat doesn't live here anymore. He moved out."

"Oh, sure."

"Get out of my face!" Davy yelled. "I told you he's gone and if you don't believe me you can roost on the front stoop for the next month and see for yourself whether he comes in or out." He slammed the door and locked it.

Then he hurried to the kitchen and searched the drawer where he knew Pat kept the weed. He'd like to roll a joint about now. But Pat had taken it with him. There were a few seeds rolling around but not enough to do anything with.

The Monopoly board still lay open on the table. It gave him the creeps. Just about everything did.

The euphoria Davy had felt from his brave decision to take the rap for Lynn's death so that Peggy might live was gone. It had been replaced in a week's time by a panic that seemed to have no ebb. No one would be lenient with him. He hadn't come forward in tears and explained that he'd committed a sudden, inexplicable act of passion which he regretted deeply. He had calmly hidden the body and told no one about it. He would be caught and severely punished, a tattooed drifter, down and out and remorseless.

Though he couldn't change it, he knew that living by himself was a mistake because it gave him twenty-four hours to brood without one human voice to interfere with his doomsday scenarios. No hour escaped the anticipation of his arrest, brutal, swift, imminent. Nothing could prevent it except Peggy's death.

He hadn't convinced her to keep her mouth shut. Maybe she'd gone with her story to the police already, her mother firmly dragging her along by the hand. In that case, why hadn't they come for him? She probably was biding her time, waiting for just the right moment to reveal the entire sad series of events. He had to stop her. Existing this way was impossible, a torture. He had to be free.

Buoyed by a bit of adrenalin, he considered new ways to kill her. He couldn't believe he was back to square one but he was. She would never again venture with him to the promontory. That much was certain. He would have to run her down with his van as she walked home from school. A hit and run solution. He'd have to pick a day fast. He could rest only when he saw her lifeless body on the street. He would do it tomorrow.

But that evening he wavered, a kite blowing north and south, then a little east and west. How could he take her life?

A wreck, he drove around town, heading nowhere in particular, just driving.

About ten o'clock he found himself out on the highway. The moon shone, a cold sphere of energy, giving lie to the myth that the night was essentially peaceful. Everywhere was turmoil, cars speeding by, radios blaring, insects splattering against the front window, planes flying low, billboards suddenly appearing out of nowhere, close to the road, painted with lurid colors made incredibly vibrant by the sudden flash of headlights.

He pulled off at an exit that turned onto a country road. He didn't know where he was or how far he was from

Freeport. It didn't matter. He was glad to be in new sur-
roundings.

Off to his right was a Baptist church illuminated by floodlights which had been wired to some surrounding trees. The
building was squat and dense, its oversized bricks painted
an ugly ochre. Davy thought it must have originally served
some secular purpose. Floodlit like that, a concentration
camp was the first association he made, but some kind of
rural government office seemed a more reasonable bet.
There was no mistaking its reincarnation — a neon cross had
been erected on its roof, the dramatic effect dimmed by the
glare of floodlights.

On an impulse he pulled into the empty lot and parked
close to the entrance. In front of him was a sign composed
of block letters under glass. The message read: GO NO
FURTHER, SINNER. YOUR PATH ENDS HERE.

If only that was so, Davy thought. He wasn't religious and
had never given God a second thought. But the idea of relaxing awhile in a sanctuary settled his nerves.

The church's interior was simple: the same ochre bricks, a
few dozen rows of wooden pews, an unadorned altar, an
overhead fan whirring fast, a string of electric lights, no floral displays.

He slid into a pew several rows back from the altar in the
shadowy recesses of which was a statue of Christ. The statue
stood about eight feet high and was carved from stone. Davy
couldn't see the face of Christ, just a mass of wavy brown hair,
windblown, flowing robes, and an outstretched hand through
which a sizable spike had been driven.

Davy sat quietly for some time, yet for whatever reason he was becoming more agitated, not less. There was no respite from the frightful decisions that were his alone to make.

He tried to rally. Why was he sitting here like a bump on a log? This was a holy place where prayers were supposed to be offered. If the path ended here, then let it, for God's sake. It had been a winding one, a real tightrope strung all the way from Tallahassee to Freeport, from an ant-filled septic tank to a moonlit cluster of deep pools.

He fell to his knees on the concrete floor and clasped his hands under his chin as images of Peggy unfolded in his mind. With a stifled cry, he prayed for her death. He prayed for her salvation. He prayed for his own death. He prayed for his own salvation. He prayed for the courage to kill. He prayed for the mercy to spare her. And above all he prayed for the total loss of his past, an unlikely miracle that nevertheless possessed him violently.

Then he left, shattered and confused, as uncertain of his master plan as ever.

He tore away from the blinding parking lot, accelerating down the country road. At the entrance to the highway the moon exposed a thicket of azaleas, pink and crimson. He sped along the highway at a fevered pitch, changing lanes erratically, blowing his horn at every vehicle that impeded his unsteady progress.

The next day saw the beginning of Davy's real decline. His mind focused on nothing. The Robotland he'd joked about to Pat was his to live in for free and for good.

He wandered through town on foot. Inching his way past

building after building like a worm. But he couldn't move any faster.

His desire to kill Peggy was gone. He didn't have the strength or the heart.

He spent his days and nights in the various fast food chains Freeport had to offer. They were all in a line on the main drag, vying for customers with blasts of neon and cheap specials. They didn't have to dazzle him. He set up shop in all of them, one after the other: Pizza Hut, Taco Bell, Wendy's, McDonald's, Burger King, Kentucky Fried Chicken. The proprietors didn't much like him but left him alone. The kids who worked behind the counters were less kind, sniggering at him and not always behind his back. He lingered over one cup of coffee after another, always making sure he had at least three packs of cigarettes with him wherever he went, for fear he'd run out if he decided to hog one stool for a lengthy stretch. The places soon smelled of his acrid smoke and there was always liquor on his breath, raising the eyebrows of fastidious parents trying to control their restless kids.

This went on for several weeks. Davy was down to less than eighty bucks. He knew it was the end.

He stared out the window into the McDonald's parking lot. Rain had begun to fall, stopping and starting fitfully.

He solemnly stirred his coffee. He guessed he'd just stay in bed tomorrow. And maybe the day after that. Maybe, he considered, he'd never get up.

That's when he overheard two girls who passed by sweeping the floor. One of them said, "Jail's too good for her. I'd like to do just the same to her as she did to that girl." The other one concurred, "She must be sick in the head."

Davy bought a paper on the way home. He protected it
from the rain by stuffing it under his shirt. He didn't mind
getting wet but wanted to keep the paper spotless. He shuffled along.

Stretched out on his bed he opened it. On page three was
an article with the headlines:

KATHY SPENCER MOVED TO
CHARLESTON CORRECTIONAL FACILITY

Then in smaller print underneath the sub-headline:

SOME CONCERNS RAISED ABOUT HER SAFETY

The detectives in charge of the case had been impressed
both by Kathy Spencer's forthrightness and her cooperation
but not by what she'd done.

She had sat before them quietly at the table, answering
their questions, sometimes taking deep breaths or pausing to
brush strands of fine blonde hair away from her eyes.

Sam Cates and Ronald Thorenson had been on the force
for ten and twelve years, respectively. Seasoned pros, they
worked as a team, wrangling the most bizarre confessions
from perpetrators with a patience Job might have envied. But
Kathy Spencer was a piece of cake. She was broken the
minute she realized her daughter was dead. No devious
questions were needed to trap her into a confession. She

wanted them to share her pain and hoped for their under-
standing.

"Tell us again, Mrs. Spencer," Thorenson said. "Tell us
what happened."

"I just told you everything."

"Try again," Cates insisted. "Maybe you left something out
that would help us figure why you acted like you did. Or
reacted as the case may be."

"Yeah," she said with bitterness. "Maybe tell you some little detail that'll keep me in prison the rest of my life. Though
I don't care much about that."

She hadn't gone so far as to request a lawyer and both men
hoped she wouldn't. They wanted to be done with the first
phase as quickly as possible. Let the lawyers, social workers,
and the media sort it all out later, as far removed from them
as possible.

"You know, Mrs. Spencer," Cates withdrew a manila enve-
lope from his desk drawer. "We have a previous file on you."

She immediately became defensive. "You do? What's it
say? I'm surprised."

The detectives had been surprised, too, although they did-
n't say so. When the report had come in the cops at the front
desk had treated it with about as much seriousness as a complaint about a barking dog. Nevertheless the complaint had
been filed, followed up, and investigated.

"It says here," Cates said tersely, "that on February 16th of
last year, a saleswoman at Sears saw you yank your daughter
so hard that she alerted security guards who held you at the
store and called the police. A patrol car was dispatched and

you were questioned by Officer Ray Petrie."

"Yes," she said. "And he let me go right there on the spot. I didn't yank her, I just grabbed her by the wrist. It's the only time something like that ever happened."

"A follow-up visit was arranged at your home," Cates continued. "A social worker named Lucy Braccio evaluated your relationship with your daughter. Apparently Mrs. Braccio found things satisfactory. She did write it up that way. But," he slowly lit a cigarette, "she was only there for two hours."

"Enough for her to see I loved my daughter and she loved me. It's true sometimes I lost my temper with her. But what mother wouldn't, if her daughter told her such an outrageous lie?"

They didn't comment.

"If once and awhile I lost my head it was only because I wanted good things for her and she wasn't getting them. . . . Do you know what it's like, waiting on a government check, your husband run out on you for good? A daughter to raise by yourself? It's scary. But," she broke into tears, "Peggy was my life. She kept me going. And now she's gone."

Cates and Thorenson exchanged glances. They pitied Kathy Spencer but their sympathies were with Peggy. They always were for the child in a case like this.

Distraught, she wailed, "I never harmed her. Ever. Don't you believe me?"

"Mrs. Spencer," Cates said. "What I believe has no relevance to anything. I'm not a prosecutor. I'm a listener. A compiler, a chronicler of unfortunate events. Somewhere down the line the information you give me I'll make available to the people who'll be involved in your case . . . Now whether they'll use it for or against you, well, I couldn't say. It's always a mystery to me."

Peggy had reached the point where she couldn't hold the secret inside her any longer. It was a millstone dragging her through the day, crushing her at night so that she couldn't get her breath and waking her up from visions of silken white arms, upraised, waving in the shadows, yearning to be touched, to be pulled from the twilight of dreams.

Kathy had fixed Peggy her favorite dinner, spaghetti with a thick tomato sauce. She'd chopped up green peppers and mushrooms and added them to the sauce and sprinkled on plenty of cheese. When she saw Peggy was only toying with the food, she was annoyed.

"Eat," she said.

"I don't feel like it."

"Are you sick?"

"Not especially."

"Not especially. What kind of an answer is that?"

They faced each other across the table. Peggy's cheeks were drained of color.

Suddenly Kathy was frightened. "What's wrong? Did something happen at school today?"

"No, Mom. Just forget it. I'll try to get the food down."

Kathy laughed, exasperated. She shook her hair out of her eyes and started gulping her food. In between mouthfuls she said, "You'll try to get it down? You got a mouth and a stomach, don't you? Shouldn't be too hard."

But Peggy left her food untouched. Troubled, she left the table and went down the three steps to the concrete porch and curled up in a rocking chair.

Kathy scraped Peggy's spaghetti into the garbage then washed their empty plates. She stood at the sink a long time, perplexed. She'd get to the bottom of this. She casually strolled out and joined Peggy. She pulled a wicker chair close to her daughter and sat down. They could barely see each other, it was so dark. Peggy wanted it that way.

"What's the matter, Miss Peggy?"

"Nothing, Mom."

"I know when something's wrong with my little girl."

"I guess you do."

"Well? Spill it."

Cringing, Peggy blurted out, "It's those arms. I see them every night coming for me. It's like she's begging me to help her."

Kathy was incredulous. "What are you playing at now?"

"I'm not playing. We have to save her. We have to rescue her. We have to let someone know she's there."

Kathy sighed. "Would you please tell me what you're talking about?"

"She's there. All by herself. In the septic tank by the woods, the one about a mile from here."

"I don't know any septic tank. I've never seen it."

"It's next to the tracks. I used to play there."

"What are you saying?" Kathy asked, miffed. "Some vagrant's living in a septic tank?"

"She's dead. Lynn. They killed her and hid her body

there."

"Who did? When?"

"Two men. A few weeks ago."

"Oh, come on. I don't believe you."

"I saw it. I was standing there. Real close. I saw them drop her body down the tank."

"That's ridiculous. Why didn't you say anything about it before?"

"I don't know . . . Maybe I was scared."

"You're making it up. Just being dramatic. You have nothing better to do than bother me with a tall tale like this." Her voice quavered. "So I'll make a damn fool of myself by calling the police and causing a big stir over nothing."

"It's true. All of it."

Her mother was petulant. "What should I expect? You don't have any friends, you don't have any dad, you make your own crazy world up and torment me with it."

Peggy jumped up. "Just leave me alone then." She stormed into the kitchen and poured herself a glass of water.

Shaken, Kathy checked her rising anger and searched for a way to give Peggy the benefit of the doubt. She followed her daughter into the kitchen. She crossed her arms.

"All right then, Miss Peggy. You saw the whole thing. What did the two men look like?"

Peggy faltered. She slowly put the glass down on the counter.

"Look at me! You say you saw the men up close. Then what did they look like?"

"I didn't — "

But Kathy cut her off cold. "You're lying."

"I don't remember . . ."

"You're lying. You wouldn't forget what they looked like. Were they young or old? Dark? Fair?"

Peggy, downcast, lowered her head. "Save her. We have to."

Kathy shook her daughter by the shoulders. "Tell me! What did the men look like? Did they have any unusual features? Any distinguishing marks? How tall were they? How were they dressed?"

Peggy saw Davy as clear as a bell, his blond hair, mustache, bandanna, and his red rose. Her shoulders sagged. Sadly she whispered, "No. I didn't see them."

"You're a liar! You torment me on purpose!"

Peggy moved away, heading for the porch. But Kathy was right behind her.

"Don't ever do it again," she screamed, furious. "Don't ever lie to me again!" And then she shoved Peggy as hard as she could down the porch steps.

Kathy heard a terrible thud.

"Peggy?" she called out.

There was no reply.

It was pitch dark on the porch. Kathy couldn't make out anything. And she was terrified to turn on the light for fear of what she might see. She went to the kitchen window and looked out. The night was choked with stars.

She got a flashlight from the kitchen drawer. It would be easier this way. She couldn't stand the shock.

Tentatively she edged down the porch steps and turned the flashlight on, angling the beam onto the porch floor.

Peggy was on her back, her eyes open, her head resting in a pool of blood. And though, mercifully, she had died right away, her lips were parted as if there were something she still wanted to tell.

The outrageous lie Kathy Spencer claimed Peggy had told was not dismissed out of hand by either Cates or Thorenson. It was their duty to investigate lies.

After the Spencer interview they drove to the area Kathy had described. Thorenson was familiar with the tank. Seven years ago it had been used as a hiding place for drugs by local teenagers.

The detectives entered the clearing and approached the septic tank but stopped a few feet away from it. It didn't take a seer to reveal a body was down there as the place was run over by huge red ants, hundreds of them, hurrying in and out of the crevices in the metal lid. Flies buzzed overhead. And a subtle smell of rot permeated the crystal clear air.

It had been a hot few weeks. Lynn's body had decomposed so that her features were beyond recognition. There had been no reports of missing women in the Freeport area, none recently in the state that matched her general bone structure or age. She would have to be put in the computer and maybe some police department somewhere would have a clue to her identity. But for now she was nameless, feature-less, an enigma.

Two new graves were dug on the hill that overlooked the

elementary school. Peggy and Lynn were laid to rest side by side. Both tombstones remained unmarked, Lynn's because no one knew her identity, Peggy's because Kathy Spencer couldn't afford an inscription, putting all her money towards making bail. She had been moved to a facility in Charleston and planned to have the tombstone inscribed as soon as she was out.

The cemetery on the hill was a lonely place. There was no one to bring flowers to Peggy or Lynn. But lilac bushes grew in profusion there, shading the tombstones from the elements and listlessly shedding their purple blossoms over the graves.

When it became clear to Davy that he was not being linked to Lynn's death, his strength returned and his damaged spirit healed. The fog he had drifted in quietly blew off and left him with a strange sense of freedom and confidence.

His apartment was no longer a dangerous cage but a comfortable home. He felt settled there and wanted to stay.

He persevered in finding work. Though it wasn't easy pickings out there, and he suffered several humiliating rejections, he eventually landed a full-time job at a lumberyard on the outskirts of town. He cut wood to builders' specifications and with his easy sense of humor and willingness to put in long hours was popular with his boss.

In fact his boss helped him open a checking account at his own bank branch, providing the reference Davy needed. There was a twinge of fear when Davy filled out the bank forms, but it didn't last for more than a minute. Why should he be afraid to reveal his name? Why should he be ashamed or uneasy about who he was? He had made a comeback of sorts and that was the cause of a stirring of pride.

On the day he cashed his first paycheck he was in a celebratory mood. It was a Friday. He had a few beers at Gavin's and bought a carton of Camels to have on hand for the weekend. All the while thinking how to celebrate his first two weeks on the job.

It would be fine to start scouting around for a new girl. God knows he could use some female companionship. But he was a little too fragile for that. Maybe by paycheck number two. He wanted to go easy. Things had a way of happening in their own time.

Evening came around. It was cooler than ususal. He closed his bedroom window. Summer was ending.

The idea came to him out of the blue. Some of the guys at the lumberyard had admired his tattoo and told him about Mike Jordan's place off the highway near the North Carolina border. Mike was a first-rate artist, they claimed. Why not let Mike do one on Davy's right arm?

Why not? What better way to celebrate?

He parked his van outside Mike Jordan's small wooden house, the roof lit up by a string of multicolored bulbs. When he knocked on the door, Jordan opened up right away.

Jordan was a wiry, affable guy, fair-skinned, about fifty. Yes, he was free now. Why didn't Davy pick something out and then he'd quote him a price? Jordan handed him a catalog to browse through, then waited on a bench against the wall which was covered with photographs of past tattoos he'd done.

Thoughtfully, Davy paged through the catalog. There were all kinds to choose from. There was a bleeding haloed Christ, there were skulls, knives, USMC, hearts, flowers, snakes.

Davy wavered. He was like a kid in a candy store. He wanted them all. But at this point he could only afford one. With some hesitation he made up his mind.

He handed the catalog back to Mike. He had decided on a vulture.